IN A WORLD OF SMALL TRUTHS

To The Watsons,
Hoping you enjoy my
"Small Truths!"
Best Wishes,
Ray

IN A WORLD OF
SMALL TRUTHS

Stories by

RAY MORRISON

Press 53

Winston-Salem

Press 53, LLC
PO Box 30314
Winston-Salem, NC 27130

First Edition

Cover design by Kevin Morgan Watson

Cover art, "Shotgun Shack," by Jeremy Miniard
Copyright © 2012 by Jeremy Miniard,
used by permission of the artist.

Author photo by Margaret Morrison

Printed on acid-free paper
ISBN 978-1-935708-67-4

For Jeni,
Who believed when I did not,
who had faith when I had none,
who nudged when I wanted to give up,
and who, as always, was right.

ACKNOWLEDGMENTS

Grateful acknowledgement is made to the following publications in which these stories first appeared:

Aethlon, "Stealing Home"
Ecotone, "Cityscape"
Word Riot, "Lenny and Earl Go Shooting Off Their Mouths"
2011 Press 53 Open Awards Anthology, "Laid to Rest"
The Mix Tape, Fast Forward Press, "S"
Press 53 Spotlight, 2010, "Allison Tarleton's Jar"
Foliate Oak, "Spring Planting"
Carve Magazine, "Shrimp Are Born Dead" (originially appeared as "Wrightsville")
Main Street Rag Press, "A House Divided"
Fiction Southeast, "The Fish"
What Doesn't Kill You... (Anthology, Press 53), "Calvin Bodenheimer and the Dalrymple Bull"
Night Train, August, 2007, "Getting the Message"
moonShine Review, "Extractions"
2010 Press 53 Open Awards Anthology, "June Bug"

In a World of Small Truths

LAID TO REST

C arson stood outside the barn and stared down at the dead dog. The coonhound's head tilted back in a wide pool of thick, clotted blood, and her red-slickened tongue drooped from a slack jaw. Carson's eyes locked on the gaping slit that ran across the dog's throat, following it from where it started underneath the exposed ear to the point it disappeared into the spongy mess below. He threw the bowl of kibble he held through the dark mouth of the barn, barely registering the clatter of the metal pan as it hit the dirt floor.

Behind Carson, the late summer sun was just cresting the ridge and the tall, dewy tobacco plants glimmered in the front field. He crossed the yard to the house. As he stepped up on the porch he smelled ham frying, which told him that Jessie was awake and in the kitchen.

He stood in the kitchen doorway watching his wife turn the thin slices of meat in the pan.

"You're up early," he said. "Is your back acting up again?"

"No, just had a bad dream," Jessie replied. "Didn't feel like staying in bed, is all."

Carson rubbed away a sheen of sweat from the back of his neck. "Dixie is dead."

Jessie turned and looked at him. He could tell she was gauging the truth of his statement.

"What're you talking about?" She stepped back from the stove and turned fully toward her husband. "How? Can you tell what from?"

Carson nodded and looked down at his boots. A smear of Dixie's blood stained the tip of one.

"Someone sliced open her throat."

"Oh, my God. Who on earth would do something like that?"

He lifted his gaze and held her eyes. Neither spoke. The ham started to smoke and Jessie flipped the knob to shut off the gas, sliding the pan off the burner.

"I think we both have a pretty good idea who did it," he said. "And I intend to do something about it."

"You don't know for sure. Don't go off half-cocked and end up doing something stupid before you've got all the facts."

"Who else would want my dog dead? You know yourself Sulley's a crazy ol' coot."

Jessie's lips tightened. "Well, I didn't until last month."

Carson nodded. He had never thought Sulley would have actually used the sledgehammer on them, that he only brought it to their house to intimidate them. Which he did well enough, especially Jessie. But now, after Dixie, Carson wondered if he'd been naïve.

"You should call the sheriff. Let him handle it," Jessie said.

"You really think Jack Mabry is going to give a shit about a dead dog? I ain't wasting my time." Carson glanced again at his boot, at the trace of blood. "I'm going out to bury Dixie now."

Carson turned and walked through to the front of the house. As he pushed open the screen door he heard the frying pan clatter in the kitchen sink.

When he reached the curing barn, the sky had brightened considerably, and the scene of his murdered dog was harsher in the clearer light. A sudden tightness seized inside Carson's chest. He stepped around the dog's body, giving a wide berth, and headed to the tool shed that sat behind the barn at the edge of the woods on the south side of his property. When he came out of the shed carrying a pickax and shovel, a jay squawked above him from a branch of a poplar tree. He paused to peer at the bird.

He picked out a spot beneath the large oak under which Dixie had spent most of her days sleeping. The ground was compact, but yielded easily enough when Carson swung the pickax hard into it. He roughed out the rectangular shape of the grave, pitching the blade into the soil over and over until the entire top layer was loosened. He paused to catch his breath and to mop his sweaty forehead with the hem of his t-shirt. He traded the pickax for the shovel and scooped the broken dirt into a pile at the base of the oak.

When he was up to his hips, Carson figured he'd gone deep enough. His shirt was soaked with perspiration and caked, along with his jeans, with red clay. Breathing hard, he gripped one side of the grave and hoisted himself out. As he brushed loose chunks of dirt off his clothing he noticed Jessie across the yard standing on the edge of the front porch watching him, her arms folded tightly across her chest. After a minute, she walked back into the house. Carson waited until his breathing slowed, rubbing at a burn that had settled into his right shoulder from the effort. When he'd got his wind back, he walked back to where Dixie's flaccid body lay. A small cloud of flies buzzed around her head and neck while others lighted atop her smudged coat. He had to straddle the puddle of dark, maroon blood in order to lift Dixie's head out of it. The hound's head flopped awkwardly and Carson reached instinctively to catch it. When he did, his fingers slid into the gaping wound on her neck.

By the time Carson carried Dixie over and laid her in the grave, it was approaching noon. He yanked off his shirt and wiped a slime of blood from his wrists and forearms before picking up the shovel to fill the hole. He lifted a shovelful of dirt from the pile and hesitated only briefly before dropping the soil on top of the dog's body. Just as Carson was patting down the last of the topsoil on the grave, Jessie came and stood at its near end and waited for him to finish. Neither of them said anything. Carson nodded once and walked over to collect the pickax from where it leaned against the oak's trunk. Without glancing back, he carried the tools to the shed. The sun burned hot on his bare back. After stowing the implements, Carson latched the door to the shed and then stepped around it to let his eyes fall on a narrow path that cut through the woods, the path that led to the wire fence marking the south border of his farm and which separated his property from Clint Sulley's.

When Carson stood on the front porch of his house the next morning he was surprised to see the thick mantle of fog that lay across the front field, so dense he couldn't make out the silhouette of his Ford pickup in the drive just off to his left. The mist brushed his bare arms, cool and moist, raising goose bumps under the thick hair of his forearms. Carson hadn't thought about the possibility it might be chilly that morning, distracted as he was by his plans. He considered going back inside to grab his jacket, but knew the sun would be rising soon and that it would almost certainly start burning off the fog before he'd even reached Sulley's place.

Carson cracked open the barrel of his shotgun to verify both chambers had shells loaded even though he'd just checked it before coming outside. When he snapped it closed, the sound echoed dully in the humid, hazy air. He patted the back pocket of his jeans to make sure the flashlight was still there.

He lingered on the top step and looked toward the expanse of the front field, invisible in the gloomy fog. He'd planned that morning to begin the summer's first cutting, and still harbored hope he could settle this thing with Sulley in time to make decent progress. At last, he stepped off the porch and toward the path, well-worn and familiar.

Carson clicked on the flashlight in order to navigate the path.

He trained the beam of light along the ground so he wouldn't trip over a root or an unexpected pit in the ground. Carson could hear small animals skittering in the leaf litter around him and the chatter of startled squirrels in the branches above. His nostrils filled with the heavy, damp smell of the dense vegetation.

Carson tried to focus on how he'd plan to approach Sulley, but a jumble of other thoughts distracted him. Try as he might, he couldn't ignore the uneasy feeling he got remembering the argument he'd had with Jessie as he dressed that morning. In all of their twenty-two years together, Carson could count on one hand the number of times he'd seen his wife cry, and most of those had been shortly after the doctor had informed them she'd never be able to have children. So it was difficult for Carson to rid his mind of the image of her sitting on the edge of the bed, amid the rumpled sheets, yelling that he was about to make a huge mistake, that she feared Sulley, a tear sliding down her freckled cheek. It was the closest he'd come to abandoning his plan, but he told Jessie this wasn't about a grudge by a sentimental man who'd lost his favorite dog, but about the bigger principle of protecting their property and not being intimidated by the likes of Clint Sulley.

Close by, a rooster crowed and its jagged yawp startled Carson. The sky was lightening and the path ahead began to appear like a developing photograph. Carson shut off the flashlight and shoved it back into his pocket. He switched the shotgun to his other hand, the metal warm and damp where he'd been gripping it.

Whether from the nebulous light or the distraction of his thoughts, Carson nearly ran into the welded wire fence separating his land from Sulley's. Standing at the fence he felt his pulse hammering in his ears. Across a wide mown field he saw the dark silhouette of Sulley's house, a light glowing dully from one upstairs window. Carson canvassed his neighbor's property, his head arcing slowly from right to left. Back behind the house he could just make out the clapboard lean-to that housed the hutches which Sulley used for raising rabbits. Not long after that stretch where a dozen or so rabbits were found torn up, some with their heads missing, Clint Sulley had seen Dixie running in his field, so he'd fixed in his mind the idea that the coonhound was guilty of attacking the animals. One evening after suppertime, Sulley had come by Carson's place to voice his accusation, armed with the sledgehammer.

A shadow moved across the shade of the lighted window. The profile was slight, reaching barely halfway up the window, so Carson assumed it was Marie, Clint's wife. Although they'd lived side-by-side for more than twenty years, the two families never became friends. In the early years, Jessie would stop by with a banana loaf or pecan pie she'd made, but the Sulleys made no effort to reciprocate, not inviting the Carsons into the house even once, and after a while Jessie quit trying. Clint and Marie Sulley had, in fact, been rarely seen off their place in the past five or six years, ever since their only child, a daughter, had run off at seventeen to marry a boy over in Stoneville.

Carson reached across the chest-high fence and propped the shotgun against the opposite side while he hoisted himself up. The fence wire swayed wildly when he lifted his weight onto it, and Carson thought he was going to flip over but he managed to hang on until he could get both legs across and hop to the ground. His right knee throbbed from the jump, a painful reminder to Carson that he was no longer a young man. He retrieved the shotgun, and marched across the dewy grass toward the house.

The rickety front porch boards moaned under Carson's weight. He pulled open the flimsy screen door and knocked. Soon he could hear the sound of heavy footsteps thumping down a staircase not far beyond the foyer. When the door opened, Clint Sulley stood nearly filling its frame. Sulley had been an all-county linebacker in high school, and although in twenty years he had softened around the middle, he was still imposing. He stood a full head taller than Carson, with massive shoulders that had undoubtedly intimidated many a quarterback back in the day. Sulley's face was covered with an ample beard, thick like fur, which extended down his neck and disappeared beyond the collar of his undershirt. The only things that were small about Clint Sulley were his eyes. They were dark, like a rodent's, and they looked down at Carson with obvious surprise.

"What is it?" Sulley asked.

Carson noticed the big man's eyes had locked on the shotgun dangling from his hand. Carson lifted the weapon, grasping the barrel with his left hand, angling it across his body.

"I reckon you know why I'm here, Clint," Carson said.

"Well, you'd be reckonin' wrong then. Why don't you tell me."

"It's about Dixie, my dog, and what you done to her yesterday."

"Your dog?" Sulley scratched at the whiskers on his cheek. "And what exactly is it I supposedly done to her?"

"You know damned well you snuck onto my property and sliced her throat. All because you got it in your head she killed those rabbits of yours."

The two men eyed each other and Carson tried to read Sulley's face, but the heavy beard made it impossible.

"I'd rather not get the law involved," Carson added. "I just want to know what compensation you are willing to make. We had that dog a long time and she was pretty special to both me and Jessie." Carson flexed his fingers to stop from gripping the shotgun so tight. "Like I told you, Dixie had nothing to do with killing your rabbits."

Before Sulley could respond, Marie's voice hollered from inside the house asking who was at the door.

"It's Mr. Carson, from across the way," Sulley called back, his eyes shifting to meet Carson's.

"What's he want?" Marie answered.

"Says someone killed his dog. He thinks I done it."

There was a long pause then and Carson thought the woman had not heard her husband.

"Oh, no," Marie said finally, her voice so quiet now that Carson almost didn't hear it.

"Please leave now," Sulley said. "You're trespassing. And from the looks at that gun, you're threatening me, too. Way I figure it, I'm within my rights to defend myself." The big man crossed his arms across his wide chest.

"I ain't leaving until we settle this thing fair and square. I'm not looking for trouble, Sulley. But what you did was crossing the line in my book."

Just then, sounds of a commotion came from inside the house and when Sulley turned to check what was going on, Carson could see Marie halfway down the stairs struggling to hold back a young boy who was clearly attempting to get down to the main floor. Even at a distance, with a limited view, Carson could tell something was not right with the child.

"Get back to bed, Robby, please," Marie pleaded. "Mommy will make you French toast if you do."

The boy was too strong for Marie to constrain. He broke past her to run down the stairs, over to where Sulley and Carson stood. Sulley bent and grabbed the boy's arm to catch and restrain him. Up close, Carson could see that the boy, whom he guessed was no more than nine or ten years old, had several physical deformities. The back of the boy's skull bulged, as big as a melon, and one eye, twice as large as the other, stared up at him dully. The boy's lower jaw hung open, his tongue protruding lazily from his mouth.

Sulley spoke softly to the boy in a voice that belied his massiveness. "Robby, be good and listen to your mother now and go on upstairs."

Robby rocked against his father's grip and seemed not to hear the command. After almost a full minute where no one spoke, the boy stopped rocking and stood still, his chin dropping against his small chest.

"I didn't realize you had a son, Sulley," Carson said, breaking the silence.

"Ain't no one's business that we do," Sulley said. "And we'd like to keep it that way." He loosened his hold of the boy's arm and then wrapped his arm around Robby's shoulders, pressing the child against him.

Suddenly, Robby jerked away from his father and began to swing his arms rapidly, his closed fists pinwheeling punches into Sulley's chest and gut. When Sulley stepped back to move away from the attack, Robby ran to him and began to bite his father's arm with sharp, crooked teeth. Sulley winced, but made no sound. He reached down, struggling to pull the boy off him. From the stairs, Marie cried out.

Outside, Carson leaned the shotgun against the house beside the door and hurried in to help. He grabbed Robby's waist and tugged him away, surprised at the strength in the boy's wiry frame.

Blood trickled from an arc of puncture wounds on Sulley's arm, but the big man didn't seem to notice his injury as he came over to where Carson struggled with the flailing child. Robby had begun screaming, a high-pitched, bestial howl that unnerved Carson. Sulley grasped both of Robby's arms and pulled him fully against his body, encircling his enormous arms around the boy and pressing him tight there until, several long minutes later, the boy had calmed down and quit struggling.

During the time that her husband soothed their son, Marie made her way downstairs and stood next to Carson. Her skin was pale and pasty, and she appeared to have lost a good deal of weight since Carson had seen her last. Up close, Carson could see the white edge of a large bandage on her neck, poking from the collar of her housedress. There were rows of red scratches on one forearm. She clasped her bony hands, rubbing each in turn restlessly, and looked up at Carson.

"He's getting worse," she said. "More violent, I mean. And awhile back he took to wandering, so now we try to keep him confined. Sometimes he escapes, though. The doctors don't know what to do. Lord knows he's takin' enough medicines to choke a mule."

Sulley gave her a sharp look, but then looked away.

"I'm so sorry," Carson said. "I'm sure they're doing all they can for him."

"I suppose," Marie replied, nodding. "They keep wanting us to put him in a special hospital. An assisted-care facility is what they call it."

Carson saw Sulley glare at his wife and shake his head. All the while he stroked Robby's hair until the boy's eyes closed, his arms going limp at his sides.

"Now, Clint, you know yourself Robby's getting to where we can't care for him proper anymore," Marie said. "We have to lock him in his room at night so he don't hurt himself."

"That's enough, Marie," Sulley said.

Marie ignored her husband and looked up at Carson, who could see that her lip had begun to quaver.

"Or hurt anyone else, either. It took us awhile, Mr. Carson, but we figured out it was Robby here who'd killed Clint's rabbits. Even chopped off some of their heads and hid them in his room. I only found out when I smelled 'em one day about a week later."

There was a long silence as Carson looked in turn from Marie to Clint and, last, to Robby, whose breaths had become so slow and deep that Carson figured the boy had fallen asleep standing against his father.

"We know what we got to do," Marie said, breaking the silence. "Don't we, honey?" She looked then at her husband, who continued to stare at the top of his son's head. "It's doing it that's the hard part."

Clint Sulley scooped his son into his arms and Robby dangled limp, like a rag doll, reminding Carson uneasily of Dixie when he'd carried her to her grave.

"I'm putting him back in bed now," Sulley said. "I didn't kill your dog, Carson. If you want, though, we can talk later. About compensation, I mean."

Carson met Sulley's eyes and he struggled to find words, but none came. Marie began to cry softly, covering her face with her hands. Finally, Carson shook his head.

Carson walked out of the house, collected his shotgun and headed across the yard toward the fence and the path through his woods. The fog had mostly cleared and the sun peeked above Clint Sulley's barn to his right. Already he could feel its warmth on his bare arms, promising a hot day ahead.

When he emerged from the woods back at his own farm, Carson headed straight to the house, glancing once at the slight mound of loose dirt near the oak tree. The leaves of the tobacco plants in the front field, still damp from the morning's heavy mist, gleamed like a thousand emerald arms, each waiting for an embrace. Carson found Jessie sitting at the kitchen table, smoking a cigarette, the first one he'd seen her smoke in years.

"It's settled," he said.

Jessie paused, the cigarette halfway to her lips. He saw her eyes scan him up and down, checking for damage. She was in her nightgown, her hair still uncombed and tangled from bed. When she looked at him, with fear and worry plain on her face, he was able to glimpse for the first time the old woman she would one day become.

"And?" she asked. Her lips tightened.

"Sulley didn't kill Dixie. I'm sure of it. You were right."

"So, now what?"

Carson pursed his lips and studied his boots for several long seconds before meeting his wife's eyes.

"We'll probably never find out who killed her, I suppose."

"Dixie was as fine a dog as ever lived," Jessie said. "It's not fair, honey."

"I know. But who said life's fair?"

Jessie stubbed out the cigarette on a saucer and stood.

"You want me to cook you some eggs?" she asked. "You haven't had breakfast."

"Sure. That'd be good. Then I need to get to cutting the front field."

Jessie walked over and put her arms around Carson and kissed him lightly on the lips. She went to the refrigerator to get the eggs and butter. As she started cooking his breakfast, Carson walked back outside and sat on the top step of the front porch. He thought about the unexpected events of the morning and of the chores waiting for him. He noticed the shotgun still leaning against the railing where he'd left it on the way in the house. He stood and took up the gun, staring at it for a long time. At last, he cracked it open and removed the shells. He lay the shotgun back against the rail and walked down off the porch. Without hesitating, Carson cocked his arm and threw the shells as far as he could, watching them arc across the cloudless, crystal blue sky until they fell lost among the waiting tobacco plants.

ALLISON TARLETON'S JAR

I was thirteen the first time I saw Allison Tarleton's uterus. Her son Dewey was my best friend, and I had come to his house after school, to hang out and play video games.

"Hello, Ridge," Mrs. Tarleton said when I walked through the kitchen door. "I want to show you something."

Dewey's mom sat at a squat Formica table, smoking, drinking a Pabst Blue Ribbon, and reading the *National Enquirer*. She and my mother were both forty-two, but Allison Tarleton looked much younger. Her hair was a deep, rusty red and tied in a ponytail that tapered to a point three-fourths of the way down her back. Augmenting her youthful appearance was the fact that her wardrobe seemed to have gotten stuck somewhere around 1970. It was common to find her wearing a dashiki shirt and tight, white bell bottoms. Allison Tarleton rarely wore shoes.

Mrs. Tarleton stubbed out her cigarette and stood slowly, pushing both palms against the red-and-orange-swirled tabletop. Crossing the room, she leaned forward, as if top-heavy, one hand pressed against her belly.

"You okay, Mrs. Tarleton?" I asked. "Dewey told me you were in the hospital, but he said it was no big deal."

"I guess to a man it *isn't* a big deal." She gave a short laugh that caused her to wince. "I had a hysterectomy." From the living room, I could hear the high-pitched sound of Space Invaders. "Do you know what a hysterectomy is, Ridge?"

"Not really," I said, meaning not at all.

"Well, let me show you." She pursed her lips, let out a long breath, then hobbled over to a cabinet. She opened it, pushed aside cans of lima beans and corn niblets, and lifted out a large pickle jar. "This is my uterus," she said, extending it to me.

Floating in cloudy fluid was a wrinkly pink blob. I knew from health class that a uterus is where babies grow, but it was creepy knowing this particular one had come out of the woman standing in front of me. Looking at the jar made me think of the time Dewey and I paid to see the freak show at the Jackson County Fair. Figuring we'd see all sorts of creepy, live oddities of nature like the Elephant Man, we were disappointed to discover a table lined with jars containing shriveled specimens of two-headed piglets and five-legged calf fetuses.

"Dewey lived in this for nine months," Mrs. Tarleton said. "But all the straining I had to do to push him out weakened the muscles holding it in place. After years of barely hanging on, they finally gave out. Two weeks ago the damned thing nearly slid clean out." She was grinning when I looked up from the floating mass. "You should've seen the look on the doctor's face when I asked him if I could take it home. 'Course, they sealed it up in some container that no one could see into, so I put it in this jar."

"That's, um, really cool, Mrs. T. I'm gonna go see what Dewey's doing." I was afraid she might open the jar and ask if I wanted to touch it.

"Well, anytime you want to see it, let me know."

"Sure thing."

I hurried to the living room where Dewey sat cross-legged on the floor in front of the television zapping Space Invaders, his eyes flitting back and forth like he was about to have a seizure.

"Hey, Ridge," he said. He didn't look away from the game.

The only parts of his body that moved were his eyes and thumbs. "Mom show you her thing?"

"Yeah. Disgusting. She said it's where you came from. I guess that explains a lot."

Dewey chuckled, still focused on the game. I sat down next to him.

"I'm on level nineteen," he said. "You'll never beat that."

He glanced at me then, to gauge my reaction to his challenge, but, when he did, the electronic aliens destroyed his ship and the game ended.

"Ha. Loser," I said. "You can't concentrate enough to be better than me."

"Okay, big mouth, show me." He threw the controller at me, hitting my shoulder.

"I don't have to." I flung the controller back at him, but he ducked and it missed. He leaped at me and we wrestled on the floor, laughing and yelling, until Dewey's mom came into the room to make us stop.

I didn't think of Allison Tarleton's uterus again for years, until one day I walked into the kitchen to find my wife at the sink, peeling potatoes. Her back was to me and her head drooped, but her shoulders hitched in an unmistakable rhythm.

I hurried to her. "Livvie, what's wrong?" A half-peeled potato dangled from her left hand, the peeler in her right. A strong earthy odor rose from the curled strips of skin that littered the sink.

"Dr. Carroll called with the biopsy results."

For over two years we'd been trying to have a baby. When at first we didn't conceive, Olivia bought a dozen books and tried everything they suggested. She kept a daily diary of every aspect of her body's condition—weight, temperature, menstrual cycle—so that she could predict the optimum time for us to have sex. I was at Barnes & Noble one day when my cell phone rang. "Get home now! My temperature's ninety-nine."

Then followed a string of doctor visits and a battery of tests. My sperm count and quality were checked first, but I was fine. Next came Olivia. Hormone levels were monitored, hormone injections were given, dye studies were conducted to check the patency of her ducts.

Then the pain started.

Initially, the doctors thought Olivia's abdominal discomfort was a side effect of the drugs they'd given her to improve the receptivity of her fallopian tubes to my sperm. But when the pain became severe, Dr. Carroll scheduled an ultrasound. The growth inside her uterus was the size of a golf ball, he said. Most likely benign, but a biopsy would tell us for certain.

"What did he say?" I felt my stomach buck.

"He said, 'It's low-grade at this time.'"

"What does that mean?"

"What the fuck do you think it means? It's cancer." She threw the potato and peeler into the sink, the spud bouncing back out. It rolled across the floor, but neither of us moved to pick it up. Olivia collapsed against the counter, burying her face in her arms.

I felt frozen. She was only thirty-one. We'd been married for five years, together for ten. Cancer was not in our plans. Surely they'd made a mistake.

"What do we do now?" I asked. I was shaking as I wrapped my arms around her. Cold and heavy, they vibrated against her back.

"Dr. Carroll said we could talk about chemotherapy, but the best hope for cure is a hysterectomy."

"Then that's what we've got to do."

She pulled back and looked up at me. Wide red bars, like war paint, ran across her cheeks from where she'd leaned against her arms. "But we'll never have children, Ridge. Never."

I started to speak, but I knew nothing I could say would matter, so I just held her again. The heat from her anger and tears burned through my shirt. We both cried then; me, because

I was afraid she'd say no to the surgery, Olivia, because she knew she wouldn't.

I held Olivia in the kitchen until she was cried out. While I stood there digesting this unexpected turn of events, my wife's hot, moist face pressed on my chest, I found myself thinking about the pickle jar in Allison Tarleton's kitchen.

It seems obvious now that Dewey and I would have been such close friends. We were similar in ways that made us different from most kids in Sylva, or any of the small towns in western North Carolina. Neither of us liked to hunt or play sports. I liked reading and writing stories; Dewey spent most of his time practicing piano and playing video games. Plus, we both had one alcoholic parent.

I can't remember ever seeing Dewey's mom without a drink. She would start in the morning with beer, then after four in the afternoon switch to vodka. But she was a tolerable drunk. The drunker Allison Tarleton got, the sillier she became. She'd giggle a lot, hug total strangers, and do crazy things like show her uterus to people. Which was a damn sight better than how booze affected my father.

Although I don't recall my dad drinking before five o'clock, except on weekends, he was more efficient than Mrs. Tarleton. His drink of choice was a brownie, three fingers of rye straight up. "Fix me a brownie, son," he'd say if I was in sight when he came home from selling—or *trying* to sell—Fords up in Waynesville. It was his version of hello. But unlike Dewey's mother, each successive drink my father took dissolved a layer of the fragile restraint he worked at maintaining throughout the day. I learned that by the end of Dad's second brownie I'd better stay out of sight or he would find some reason to yank off his belt and whip me.

My mother often acted as my sentry. "Why don't you go up to your room and read a book, Ridge, and let your father unwind. He's especially tired tonight." Too often, though, I would sit on my bed, my legs tucked tight against my chest, and listen as she ended up taking the brunt of his anger.

During the summer, whenever Dewey wasn't practicing the piano, or trouncing me at Asteroids or Centipede or Space Invaders, we'd hike into the woods or, more often, ride our bikes down to the Tuckasegee River to sit for hours on the big rocks pressed into its banks. Dewey insisted we ride for several miles along the sloping verge, beside the railroad tracks that followed the river's course, until we came to a tight horseshoe bend in the water. Here, the river was edged by tall basswood and ash trees that cast black shadows across the water. In this secluded spot, the crook in the river tempered the already languid flow to create a pool where we could jump from the rocks and swim. On the hottest days, Dewey would strip off all his clothes and cannonball into the water, coaxing me to do the same. When exhausted from swimming, he'd lie on a large, flat rock in dappled sunlight, his hands twined behind his head, and let the hot summer air dry him. I would scramble up, self-conscious in a way he never was, wiggle my underpants over my wet, clinging skin, then lie beside him. In those hours, we would have deep discussions about everything or about nothing; solve every problem, solve nothing.

Dewey was a year older than me, and the year his mom had her hysterectomy was his final year at Smokey Mountain Elementary. I still had eighth grade. One afternoon in late June, not long after school ended, we lay on our river rock, dripping puddles into the cracks and crevices of the hot granite.

"Well, it's high school for me next year," Dewey said.

I waited, but he didn't say more. I turned my head toward him. His eyes were open, fixed on the baked, cloudless sky. His damp skin, white and thin, looked as if it would tear if you touched it. With his arms stretched above him, I could see the parallel lines of his ribs pushing out.

"It's gonna seem funny not riding the bus with you," I said.

"Aw, you'll survive."

"Yeah, but you said you were gonna flunk this year so we could go to high school together."

Dewey smiled. He reached over and patted the top of my head. "Ridge, my friend, time waits for no man. Time heals all wounds. There's a time to every purpose under heaven. There's a time and place for everything. Time flies. Why, time . . ." He stood up, naked, propped his hands on his hips, poked out his lower lip, and proceeded to do the worst Mick Jagger imitation ever. "Ti-i-i-ime is on my side, yes it is. Oh, yeah . . ."

I slapped at Dewey's legs, but he danced out of my grasp. When I latched onto his ankle, he reached down to pry my fingers off, but I gripped tighter and rolled away, giggling. We wrestled for a moment, but he was stronger and pinned me. Dewey knelt straddling me, grinning. Abruptly, I stopped laughing. He must have sensed my unease and rolled off. When he saw my mouth was agape, he looked down and noticed his erection. He jerked his own shorts on and we rode home. Neither of us mentioned it again.

Sam Carroll was a tall, muscular man whose private office was a comfortable oasis from the cold sterility of the rest of his gynecology practice. When he wasn't delivering babies, or throwing people's lives into a tailspin with unexpected cancer diagnoses, he was a competitive swimmer. Photographs of him standing next to a pool wearing a Speedo, his shaved head gleaming, hung on the wall behind his desk. He was the only middle-aged man I knew who was bald by choice. His most interesting feature, however, was his voice. When you first met him, you expected to hear a deep, imposing voice, one as big as the man. But Carroll's voice was soft, nearly hypnotic in its ability to soothe and console. On our visits after Olivia's diagnosis, I often found myself leaning forward to hear him.

"Any questions?" Carroll asked. Olivia's hysterectomy was scheduled for the following day and he'd explained the surgical procedure in detail.

Olivia and I looked at each other, shook our heads. I was relieved to learn that there wasn't going to be any incision on the outside, so Livvie wouldn't have a scar.

Early the next morning we drove to the hospital and met Dr. Carroll and his nurse in the receiving area. He assured us again how common the procedure was and, barring any surprises, Olivia would be home by dinnertime the following day. The nurse put her arm around Olivia's shoulders and guided her down a long hallway. Just before they passed through a set of tall swinging doors, Livvie turned. She lifted her hand to me, her eyes wide and frightened.

"She'll be fine, Ridge," Carroll said. "We'll check the tissue carefully to make sure we get all of the malignancy. Try not to worry. As soon as we're done, I'll be out to let you know how things went."

"Yes." I didn't know what else to say.

I ambled into the waiting area, which was deserted. A TV mounted near the ceiling was tuned to the *Today Show*. The volume was so low I could make out only every third or fourth word. I watched a shot of the crowd on the sidewalk outside the studio. People were waving homemade signs to friends back home. A plump woman with bright orange hair held one that read, "Howdy, North Carolina!" I waved at the television and said howdy back.

I thumbed through a magazine, scanning the pictures. A thought kept interrupting, breaking my concentration—I'd always expected to bring Livvie to this hospital to deliver our baby, not to make it impossible for her to have it.

It was during my second year at the University of North Carolina that my mother called to tell me my father had cancer. Unlike Allison Tarleton, who would keep her alcoholism like a trusted friend into old age, my dad had stopped drinking two years before my freshman year. When Mom gave me the news, she mentioned that Dad's spirits were good. She assured me that they were doing everything possible. He'd already had a radiation treatment, and was on three different chemo drugs, including an experimental one not yet approved by the FDA. I offered to come home, but Mom insisted I stay at school.

Arriving home for Thanksgiving break, I was shaken by my father's appearance. He looked like someone had jammed a hose into his body and sucked half his insides out. His skin hung in swags on his bones. When I walked into the house he was lying on the living room sofa. The room was hot and permeated by the faint, sour smell of vomit. I was unable to hide my shock.

"Surely I don't look that bad, do I?" he said.

"No, it's just . . ."

"That's okay, Ridge. There are mirrors in the house." He laughed, short and harsh, which led to a coughing fit. He leaned over and spit into a small trash can parked beside the couch. The spit was dark red.

"You okay?" I asked. The question was stupid. I had no idea what to say.

"As good as can be expected." He wiped a smear of bloody mucus off his chin with a tissue. "Mom's in the backyard, in her garden. She's waiting for you."

"Dad, I . . ."

"Go on, now," he said. He waved his thin, pallid arm toward the back of the house. "I need to rest. We'll talk later."

My mother was kneeling in the long rectangular garden that ran the length of the house's back wall. I stood for a moment and watched as she scooped handfuls of fresh, dark potting soil from a plastic bag and sprinkled it around a patch of purple and white chrysanthemums. A sharp wind snapped the flaps of my jacket, so I zipped it up and stuffed my hands into the pockets. My mother wore only a thin brocade sweater over her house dress, with a silk scarf covering her head. I could tell she, too, had lost weight.

"Beautiful," I said.

She straightened and looked at the mums. "Yes, they are."

"I meant you." She smiled and gave me a dismissive wave. "But don't you think it's too cold to plant flowers, Mom?"

"Oh, mums are hardy." She looked along the row she'd planted, but I saw the doubt in her eyes. "I'll tend to them; they'll do well enough for a while. In any event, Ridge, I'll enjoy them as long as I can."

"If anyone can keep them going, it's you, Mom."

"Here, help me up, you cheap flatterer. Did you see your father?"

"Yes. He's taking a nap."

"Good. He's not been sleeping well." I held her elbow to steady her as she stood. She wiped soil from her spade, and then removed her gloves.

"How bad is it?" I asked. "How long?"

My mother was tall, and when she turned to look at me, we were eye-to-eye. She took a deep breath, let it out slowly, then hooked her arm through mine and led me away from the house, out to a bench that encircled a massive oak tree in the middle of the backyard. The bench's white paint was cracked and chipped and graying. My father had built it when I was five. He'd ask me to hand him tools as he needed them, teaching me their names and what they were for.

We sat on the far side, the oak tree hiding us from the house, looking west toward the indistinct rise of the mountains of the Nantahala Forest, whose foliage was past peak of color, but still beautiful.

"I don't understand how he could've changed so fast," I said. "When I left for school, he looked fine."

"It's not just the disease, Ridge. It's the treatments, too. They're hard on him." She turned from me to look at the hills. "I just wish they were working."

"What do the doctors say?"

"What *can* they say? They're trying, but it spread fast. Yesterday a new scan showed the cancer had moved to his brain. They talked about operating, but we decided against it." She turned to me, picked up my hand and covered it with hers. "We need to make the best of the time we have left. It's what he wants."

"What can I do?" I asked.

She leaned over and kissed my cheek. "Come help me with dinner."

My mother stood and walked back to the house, leaving me alone on the bench. I picked at a flake of paint, peeling it off, flicking it onto the grass. I stared down at the curl of paint and thought of the drunken beatings, the weekends spent at Dewey's house to avoid my father, the years of watching my parents fight. But mostly I thought about the past two years, the sober years, and how I'd just begun to glimpse the man my father must have been, the man my mother fell in love with. How I liked that man and had looked forward to spending time with him.

I sat out there a long time, until my mother called me to dinner and the light had leached from the sky, turning the mountains into dark, gray ghosts in the distance.

Except to go to the bathroom, my dad stayed on the sofa the four days I was home. He was weak from the chemo; he'd experience vertigo if he wasn't lying down. Mom and I ate Thanksgiving dinner on flimsy aluminum TV trays next to the sofa. Dad couldn't hold solid food down, so he just watched us.

I left on Sunday after fighting with my mother about staying. In the end it was my father who insisted I go back, saying I needed an education more than I needed to watch him puke all day. Besides, Christmas break was only three weeks away. So I loaded my VW and made the five-hour drive back to Chapel Hill. As soon as I'd arrived, I saw the note tacked to my dorm door. "Ridge, Call your mother. URGENT!" I didn't even go into my room. I phoned my mother, and then drove back to Sylva.

I didn't make it in time. I was sitting on an uncomfortable vinyl chair in the waiting room of the oncology wing at Jackson

Memorial Hospital when my mother came to tell me he'd died, but that it was a blessing.

Three days later we buried him in a small cemetery at the foot of Carver Mountain, and I saw Dewey Tarleton for the last time.

After Dewey started high school, I'd still go to his house after school. His bus got home later than mine, so often I would get to his place first. His mother was always at the kitchen table, drinking, smoking, and leafing through gossip magazines.

"Hi, Ridge, there's Cheerwine in the fridge if you want some."

"Thanks."

Often, her womb jar would be sitting on the counter next to the refrigerator. I thought about asking her why she kept taking it out, but even as a teenager I realized I didn't really want to know.

I'd take a can of soda into the living room and power up the Atari. Half an hour or so later, when Dewey got home, we'd play for a while. But as the school year wore on, more often than not, he'd say he had a ton of homework and head up to his bedroom. I'd hop on my bike and ride home to sit in the eye of the hurricane until my father arrived.

After Christmas that year, Dewey joined several school clubs, so he wouldn't get home until after five o'clock. It was an awkward time for me and one of the loneliest periods of my life. I became aware of how much I depended on Dewey. My mother noticed that I wasn't spending as much time at his house and told me not to worry, that the following year I'd be in high school, too, and we'd be together like before. Besides, she reminded me, we had the whole summer.

Of course, when summer arrived things weren't like before. Dewey began to spend time with two boys from the drama club. He and I would still hang out together, but it was never the same. Only once, near the end of summer, did we ride our bikes out to our private spot by the river. It was bright and hot, over ninety, but I could hear thunder rumbling in the distance, over the mountains. The smooth, hard surface of the rock was too hot to lie on, so we just sat with our legs pulled up to keep our bare skin off the stone. Neither of us took off our shirts or shorts. We didn't swim.

"Hot as hell, but feels kinda good," Dewey said after a long silence.

"Yeah, I guess."

"I've been meaning to tell you something, Ridge." I waited. "I applied for admission to the School of the Arts in Winston-Salem, to their high school, so I can study drama. Yesterday I got a letter saying I got in."

"You're leaving Sylva?"

"Jack's going there, too." Jack was one of his new best friends. "I'll be staying with his aunt and uncle."

We stayed at the river another hour or so, but we didn't talk much. I listened as the thunder got closer and watched the shadows of clouds shade the surface of the Tuckasegee. When the first fat drops of rain fell we rode home, making it back just before the downpour.

The day before Dewey left for Winston-Salem, he came to my house to say goodbye and bring me a gift.

"I thought you'd want this. I won't have time to use it." He handed me the Atari console, four or five bulky game cartridges sliding across the top. "*Now* maybe you'll be able to beat me."

I held the game system at arm's length, like it was radioactive. "Thanks, Dewey."

"Well, I have to finish packing. I wanted to give you that, and to say goodbye."

My body felt suddenly light, and the Atari too heavy to hold. Dewey looked like he wanted to say more, but just reached out and put his hand on my shoulder, squeezing hard. "Well, I gotta go. See you at Christmas, Ridge."

I struggled to speak, like the words were attached to my throat with fingers that wouldn't let go. "Yeah. Thanks for the games."

I did see Dewey a couple of times during school breaks, but by the next summer he was staying in Winston-Salem full-time. We wrote each other occasionally, and I found other friends in high school, but by the time I graduated and made plans to go to UNC, we'd gone our separate ways. I'd see Dewey's mother in town—at the Food Lion or the drugstore—and she'd give me updates on what he was doing or what play he was appearing in, but when my father died, it had been four years since I had seen him.

When Dewey walked into the funeral home, I didn't recognize him. His hair was long, to his shoulders, and he had a thin mustache. Although he'd always been skinny, he appeared way too thin.

"Ridge, I'm sorry about your dad," he said after hugging me.

"Thanks. I appreciate you coming." It was at this moment I noticed the red, raised, bell-shaped sore on his neck. "What happened there?" I asked, pointing.

"Don't you recognize a hickey when you see one?" He laughed, but the sound was hollow, without humor.

The next spring, during the same week I met Livvie in a journalism class, I received a letter from Allison Tarleton telling me that Dewey had died.

Livvie poked me with her elbow. "Your turn."

I rotated the knob of the baby monitor to quiet the steady shrill that had pierced our sleep. I rolled onto my back and rubbed my eyes. Olivia twisted onto her side, covering her head with her pillow. I swung my legs off the bed and sighed.

In the nursery, the baby continued his insistent wail. I bent to the crib and lifted him out, pressing his soft, warm body against my chest. His crying quieted to a rhythmic whimper. I carried him downstairs to the kitchen to warm a bottle. As I waited for the water to boil, I sat holding my new son as he drifted into a half-sleep. We'd returned from Russia just two weeks earlier and the excitement about the adoption was replaced by the exhaustion of caring for an infant.

In the dim light of the kitchen, I looked down at the top of Dmitry's fuzzy head and could see the delicate indent of his fontanelle. I stared at the dark spot, amazed at how dangerously fragile we come into this life.

"The water's boiling, Ridge." I hadn't heard Olivia come into the room. "I couldn't sleep. Let me hold Dimmy."

I handed up the baby and went to put the bottle in the pan. Olivia took my seat.

"You were right," she said.

"About what?" I swirled the bottom half of the formula in the water.

"I didn't think I'd feel the same about Dimmy as I would a baby that came out of me, but I was wrong."

After Livvie's hysterectomy, the tissue analysis showed that all the cancer had been confined to the area of the tumor. The surgery saved her life, even if it meant she'd never conceive. It had taken over a year for her to come around to the idea.

"You're going to get it too hot. Here." Livvie came over to the stove and held out the baby.

"Come here, Dewey," I said.

"Why did you call him that?"

"Call him what?"

"Dewey."

"I did?"

Olivia tested the milk on her wrist, then sat down beside me. I cradled my son in my arm and took the bottle from her. Dimmy sucked it eagerly, his eyes rolling back. I became mesmerized by the cadenced movement of his lips and cheeks. I looked up at Livvie, who smiled before reaching over to stroke Dimmy's soft hair with the tips of her fingers.

Sitting in my kitchen at three in the morning, watching my wife and son, I found myself thinking of many things—the potato which had lain forgotten under our kitchen counter for a week before we noticed it, the chrysanthemums my mother plants every year now at Thanksgiving, the moist silty odor of the Tuckasegee after I dived in.

And I thought, too, about Allison Tarleton's jar. Was it still stashed away in her kitchen cabinet, or had she thrown it away after Dewey died. I looked at Olivia and Dimmy and I knew.

STEALING HOME

My dad elbows me, and says, "My God, Joltin' Joe looks awful. His swing has gone to hell." His eyebrows are pulled down tight and he's shaking his head. There's a glob of mustard smearing his chin. I reach over and wipe it off with a napkin.

This is what he always says when we come to the ballpark now, and it never matters who the batter is or what team is playing. I'm learning not to argue with him. The first few times I would patiently explain that DiMaggio died in '99 and, besides, we were watching the Braves. A couple of years back, before the Alzheimer's got too bad, he'd consider my explanation and snap out of it for a bit, and say something like, "Oh, yeah, I meant Chipper Jones. He's swinging too early." Now I try to do what his doctors advised and just let him tell it like he sees it. But sometimes, like this afternoon, when he starts in again with the disparaging remarks about Joey D, it gets to me, so I squabble with him. I'm forty-seven years old, but his illness makes me feel twelve again.

"If he's swinging so bad, how do you explain his batting average?" I ask.

He narrows his eyes, taps his finger against his temple. "You don't think I know he's hitting .325, do you?" He gives me a you-can't-fool-me wink, and then thrusts his thumb in the general direction of home plate. "But that won't last long, he keeps this up."

Even though I inherited my impatience from my father, it still feels bad when I use it against him. I often wish I was more like my mother. Sometimes I think God sent her to him because He knew what was coming at the end, that my father would need someone like her.

The three of us were at a restaurant the other day and every time the waiter came by, Dad would complain he didn't have a spoon. "How do you expect someone to eat soup without a spoon?" he asked. The waiter would look confused and my mother would touch the waiter's arm and give him a smile. The kid would disappear into the kitchen, and then my mother would pick up the spoon resting right next to Dad's plate and hand it to him. "Here's a new spoon, dear," she said. When he took the spoon, Dad glanced down to try and figure out what he needed it for, and then put it back on the table. This was repeated over and over, and each time the waiter walked away my mother would once again offer the same utensil. By the sixth or seventh time, I'd had it. I snapped at him. "Dad, will you please stop asking for a damn spoon?"

I apologized to the waiter, but it was pointless. I knew it would happen again. And not just there. Everywhere. Later that evening, tomorrow, for as many days as we have left.

In a crazy way, I envy my father. Every repeated sentence, every repeated action, is brand new for him. Each delusion is as real and solid for him as the ground he walks on. It is, I think, the disease's only mercy.

"You know what I could go for right about now?" my father asks. "A big ol' hot dog, that's what. Nothing better than a red hot at a ballgame, Donny."

I glance at the half-eaten hot dog lying on the tray perched on his lap. I pick it up and hold it in front of him. "Here. I'm not going to finish mine, you can have it."

"You sure?" he asks, taking it from me.

The crowd boos loud and long and I turn to see that Andruw Jones has been called out on strikes to end the sixth inning.

"See there. What'd I tell you?" Dad says. His cheek is bulging with hot dog and his words are garbled. He stretches his neck toward the field and cups his hand around his mouth. "C'mon, DiMaggio! Get it together, or stay on the bench." Little wads of hot dog and bun spray out as he shouts, and a couple of men in the row below us turn and give Dad a dirty look.

"It'll be okay, Dad," I say, putting my hand on his arm and guiding him back into his seat. "He'll get out of this slump soon."

I glance out at the scoreboard clock. It's a few minutes shy of three o'clock. I decide we'll leave during the seventh inning stretch so we can beat traffic. Barring any delays, we should get back to Shelby by seven-thirty or eight.

"Hey, Donny, look at Yogi. Does he look a lot taller than usual?"

On the field, the Braves are getting set for the top of the seventh. The catcher adjusts his chest protector and then squats to take the warm-up pitches from John Smoltz.

"Dad, that's not Yogi Berra. It's Javy Lopez." But as I watch the catcher it occurs to me that Lopez was traded to the Orioles a couple of years back. The catcher's name is Johnny Estrada. I start to tell my father but he is staring out across the diamond. I figure it doesn't matter.

"Remember when I brought you here the first time?" he says. His head rotates slowly from right field to left, taking in the ballpark.

Without effort, my mind retrieves the memory. My father—handsome, muscular, younger than I am now—driving the three of us to Atlanta from North Carolina. I was seven and bouncing in the enormous back seat of our beige Rambler. My mother tried to get me to sit still, but Dad explained that it was no use because I was too excited about going to the game. He turned around and gave me a smile, like we shared a secret she could never know. And when we walked into Fulton County Stadium that afternoon, the outfield grass spreading away from me was so perfect and green—greener than any lawn back home, it was like I was finally seeing the color that God had intended for grass—and the infield dirt so smooth and brown, like sanded wood. I thought I'd never see a more beautiful place as long as I lived.

The announcer calls the name of the Phillies' batter as he steps to the plate.

Dad squints and leans forward, and his eyes look a little sad. The cardboard tray drops between his feet. "Mantle and Maris in the outfield. I'm glad I was able to take you to see them. There won't be many like them playing together."

It takes me a second to realize he is remembering our first game together as being at Yankee Stadium. A place, to this day, I've never been.

"Hey, Donny, I've got an idea," Dad says. "What say we work our way down to the field right after the game and get the two of them, and maybe Yogi if we can, to sign a ball for you?"

His eyebrows are arched and his eyes are full of expectation, waiting for my reaction to this surprise gift he's given me. Only then does it occur to me that this is our last game together.

What would it cost me? A couple hours' delay getting home? It would be easy, too. Head down to the railing after the game with a ball I'd buy at the souvenir shop, get any player—heck, maybe even the batboy—to sign it. Explain quietly what's going on and see if they'll even write the Mick's name. The rest would be a snap. The two of us oohing and aahing over our treasure—just Dad and me.

I stand. "Well, we'll need a ball, then. Let's go to the souvenir place and get one."

My father grins and grips the handles of the seat and tries to push himself up. I take his arm, thin and bony and fragile, and help him. We move down the ramp toward the dark tunnel that leads to the concourse.

As we make our way, my mind searches for the Yankees of my youth. "Hey, Dad, how 'bout after Mantle and Maris we try to get Tony Kubek to sign the ball, too?"

My father stops and jerks his arm from my hand with surprising strength. When he looks at me, I can't read his eyes, but I feel he is onto me, that his memory has cleared for a moment and he knows what I am trying to do.

"Kubek?" he says. He turns to look at the field for a moment, then takes a step closer and puts his face so close to mine that I can smell the hot dog on his breath. "You tell me you want to have Tony Kubek's signature on the same baseball as Mickey Mantle and Roger Maris?" He sighs and shakes his head. "Why, Kubek is nothing. Now, Rizzuto—*there* was a shortstop. No, son, Kubek ain't spoiling our ball."

My father heads down the ramp. I reach forward and grab his elbow and let him lead us away from the brilliant sunshine of Turner Field.

LENNY AND EARL GO SHOOTING OFF THEIR MOUTHS

Lenny leaned against the Volkswagen's window to catch a glimpse of the full moon. It hung high off the left side of the pocked gravel road, so brilliant in the hot, clear sky that it lit up the route like a searchlight. The car's right front tire dropped into a deep hole, bouncing him high enough to bang his head against the car's roof. Flakes of rust clung to his hair. He grabbed the wheel with both hands. In the passenger seat, Earl shifted and moaned, still asleep.

It was two hours since they'd crossed the North Carolina line, headed for the old cabin that belonged to Lenny's uncle. Lenny had spent his boyhood summers there, fishing and hunting the streams and woods of the Sandhills. But that was years ago.

The gravel ended abruptly and the road tapered to a dirt lane. The heavy gray dust cloud that trailed the small car changed to a thinner, orangey mist blowing up from sun-baked dirt. A sharp bend caught Lenny by surprise, and he braked hard, skidding nearly out of control. The turn brought a stark change in the landscape. No longer bordered by open, cut, late-summer fields and small farms, the road was now hemmed by tall, straight loblolly pines and scrubby vegetation. Patches of white, sandy soil glimmered in the headlights.

Lenny downshifted, slowing so he wouldn't miss the landmarks for the next turn. He shook Earl awake.

"What is it?" Earl sat up and yawned. "Where the hell are we?"

"Almost to the cabin. Help me look for the turnoff. I'm lookin' for a sign on the right, pointing down an access road, toward the river. Says somethin' like Pee Dee Watershed Management Site Number 12 or 20."

"Well, which is it? Twelve or twenty?"

"What?" Lenny was concentrating on the small headlight beams flashing across the trees.

"Will it say twelve, or twenty?"

Lenny looked over at Earl. "Hell, it could be Number 8, for all I know. What difference does it make?"

"What do you mean, it could be Number 8?"

"Earl, just look for any damned sign pointin' to any damned watershed site."

"Hey, don't get mad at me. I'm not the numbnuts can't remember what the number is. And what kinda sign did you say it is? A waterbed?"

"Water*shed*. Waterbed don't make sense."

"You ask me, this whole cabin idea don't make sense. Especially you not rememberin' what number is on the sign."

Lenny's head swiveled back and forth, from the road to the stupid grin on Earl's face, and he gripped the steering wheel until his knuckles turned white. Finally, he stomped on the brake and clutch, the small car fishtailing to a stop. He glared at Earl, who fell against the dashboard.

"Listen, asshole, thanks to you, I'm under quite a bit of pressure here. I jus' want to get to Uncle Bo's cabin so I can figure out what to do about this mess we're in." He leaned over and put his face right next to Earl's. "*Your* mess."

"Whoa, there, Len. A little too much nacho cheese, partner." Earl wrinkled his nose.

"What the fuck is wrong with you?" Lenny asked. "Ain't you got any idea of the fix we're in?"

"Sure I do. It's just that . . . well, that breath of yours is makin' it hard to think."

Lenny's fists balled up and he pulled back to throw a punch. Earl flinched, pulling his arm up in self-defense. Lenny regained control and pulled his hand down. He took a deep breath, letting it out in a slow, tight stream through pursed lips. It was an anger management technique he'd learned from his ex-wife, Gail. He often thought it was about the only good thing he'd ever got from the marriage.

"Just keep an eye out for *any* signs. Do you think you can do that?"

"Yeah, sure." Earl slowly lowered his arm. "I jus' wish I knew what number I was lookin' for."

Lenny sighed. He put the VW in gear and pointed the car back down the road. As he drove, he peeked at Earl, who spent his time picking at a dried glob on his shirt, instead of looking out the window for signs. Considering the rest of the mess on his clothes, Lenny was confused about Earl's concern with that particular stain.

Distracted by Earl, Lenny nearly missed the sign for the watershed turnoff. It turned out to be Site Number 21. "There's the sign," he said, pointing back over his shoulder. Earl turned to look.

"What number is it?"

"Twenty. Just like I said." Lenny smiled.

About a half mile beyond the access road, another road cut into the pines on the left side. Lenny misjudged how far it was past the sign, and didn't see it until he'd passed it. He had to stop and back up. Wide spaces separated the trees and a thick bed of dried, russet needles blanketed the ground in the open areas between them, including the narrow drive. The branches diffused the moonlight, creating a web of shadows all around them. Lenny carefully guided the Beetle through the forest until, at last, the cabin's dark shape appeared atop a knoll ahead of them. He parked around back.

"Get the guns," Lenny said, nodding toward the back seat. "I'll get the money and other stuff out of the trunk." He shut off the engine.

"Why can't I get the money?"

"Come again?"

"I mean, why do you get to carry the money?"

"Jesus Christ, Earl. Do you think I'm gonna run off into the woods with two big bags of stolen cash, hike fifteen miles back to Marston with them swingin' over my shoulders, stop some yokel and ask him if he knows a nice motel where I can stay?"

"Well, no, that's not what I'm saying." Earl pushed up the brim of his Durham Bulls ball cap. A greasy strand of long blond hair fell across the left side of his face. "But half that money *is* mine."

"And one of those shotguns is mine. Do you hear me saying I think you're gonna keep 'em both? I'm not planning on keepin' your money. I'm just gonna carry it inside."

"Well, then, why don't you carry the guns, and I'll carry the money?" Earl scratched his stubbled cheek.

"Godammit, Earl, you're really pissin' me off." Lenny took another deep breath, and rubbed the back of his neck. "All right. How about this? Why don't you carry one of the guns and one of the bags of cash, and I'll carry the other." Lenny watched Earl process his proposal.

"Then who carries the groceries?"

Lenny stared at Earl for a long moment. "I'm going in." He reached into the back and grabbed his shotgun, and then slammed the car door. At the front of the car, he yanked open the trunk so hard it bounced back shut, nearly clipping his head. He reopened it slowly, and hooked his fingers through the loops of four plastic grocery bags. He tucked the shotgun under his arm. With his free hand, he grabbed one of the canvas bank bags.

"Nice night, don't you think?" Earl had come up beside Lenny, holding the other gun against his shoulder like a soldier.

"Though I 'spect it's going to rain. You can smell it in the air."
He closed his eyes, tilted his head back and sniffed deeply.

Lenny shook his head and banged the trunk closed.

"Hey! I need to get the other bag out of there."

Lenny walked around to the other side of the cabin. He
stepped onto the low, covered porch and placed all of the bags
next to the door. The full moon, covered now by thin ribbons
of cloud, still provided enough light to see. Lenny studied the
porch's edge to locate a board with a deep, weathered V notched
in a corner. Counting five boards over from the V, he leaned
down and felt the ground below the porch for the key he trusted
would still be there. It was. Before unlocking the door, he dug
around in the shopping bags to find a flashlight and some
batteries. Lenny aimed the beam into the cabin, just as Earl
appeared at the side of the building.

When he walked into the one-room cabin, Lenny recoiled at
its thick, damp mustiness. He ran the light in hurried, jerky
movements—up, across, down, back up—as he scanned the
large space. In a far corner, the flashlight's beam surprised a
large rat, its perfectly round eyes shining like tiny stoplights.
The rat darted away and Lenny was just able to see its tail
disappear down a hole in the floor, beneath one of the cabin's
two windows.

"Leave the door open, so we can get some air in here."

"Jesus! This place smells worse than your breath," Earl said,
ambling up to the door. "Shine the light over here so I can see
where I'm walkin'. I don't want to step in some animal's shit."

Instead of pointing the beam at Earl's feet, Lenny aimed the
light at one of the grocery bags. "Hurry up and get the other
flashlight out of the bag."

As Earl moved about, inspecting the stuffy room, Lenny
opened a gallon water jug, poured some into each palm and
rubbed them together briskly. He dried his hands on the legs of
his jeans.

"Hey, Earl," Lenny said, holding up the jug. "You might want to see if you can get some of that blood off your hands. Though I'm not sure what we're gonna do with your clothes."

Earl was shining the flashlight down the rat hole. He stood up and walked over to Lenny. He tried the same washing technique as Lenny, but he had far more blood, too much to get all of it without soap or a towel.

"Damn, this shit is sticky." Earl's pants were too covered in blood to be used for drying, so he shook his hands rapidly to dry them. "Why the hell didn't you remember to grab soap?"

"If it wasn't for your stupidity, we wouldn't even *need* soap. Why didn't *you* think to get some?"

"All I'm sayin' is, it wouldn't have hurt you to pick up a bar of Ivory or something when you was running around like a madman, grabbing shit."

"I was only running around like a madman because, as always, you have to go and act like an idiot when you think someone looks sideways at you. There was no reason to be shootin' those people, Earl." Lenny grabbed the jug from Earl and took a drink.

"I told you. He was mouthin' off at me."

"He was not. I was standing right next to you. He never said a word."

"He muttered it under his breath. You just couldn't hear it. He called me a hippie, plain as day. But I ain't no goddamn hippie, and no one is going to call me one, either." Earl spit toward the door.

"Well, if I couldn't hear it, I don't see how you could've."

"So, you're sayin' that guy didn't say anything, and I blew his brains out for fun?"

Lenny threw his arms out wide. "That's *exactly* what I just said, asshole!" He started to take a calming, deep breath, but stopped. "Screw Gail, and screw you, Earl."

"What's your wife got to do with this?" Earl asked.

"*Ex*-wife, asshole. And she ain't got nothin' to do with this."

"Then why'd you say her name? That don't make much sense, Lenny. Like you not getting any soap."

"Will you forget the fuckin' soap, for chrissake!" Lenny pressed his fingertips against his temples and closed his eyes.

"Easy for you to say. Thanks to me, you only got a little blood on you. If I hadn't blocked most of it, you'd be soaked, like I am." Earl held his arms open in a look-at-this gesture.

"Only because *you* were the one who decided to shoot that clerk for no reason, you idiot." Lenny began pacing the small cabin. He glanced at the rat hole, suddenly wishing the rat would come back.

"I told you, he called me a goddamn hippie. Ain't no one gonna smartmouth me like that and get away with it."

"Well," Lenny said. "He sure as shit didn't get away with it."

In the reflected glow of Earl's flashlight, Lenny saw the other man was smiling at what he'd thought was a compliment.

"But I still think you were an idiot not to have snatched some soap," Earl said.

Lenny stopped pacing and shone his flashlight directly in Earl's face.

"Hey, get that out of my eyes."

Lenny hands were shaking, but he managed to keep the light pointed at Earl's face. He backed up to where his shotgun leaned against the wall. Waving his hand behind him, he felt the gun's barrel. He lifted it and aimed it at Earl.

"What are you doin', Len?"

"I'm gonna ask you to do something that I ain't so sure you're capable of doing, Earl. I want you to shut up."

Earl backed away slowly. "Sure thing, Lenny. I'll shut up. I ain't got no problem with that. If that's what you want me to—"

"*Shut up, now!* And don't move." The gun wobbled in Lenny's hands. "I've had just about all of you I can take, Earl. We had it made, can't you see that? Hittin' that restaurant went just as I planned. We got the money from the safe and got away without anyone even seein' us. All we had to do was head out west and enjoy the money. But you couldn't be cool with that, could you?"

"Lenny, listen, man . . ."

Lenny cocked both barrels. "This is your last warning, Earl. Don't say another fuckin' word."

Earl held his palms out, nodded and smiled. Casually, he tucked his thumbs into the waistline at the back of his jeans.

"I wish to hell I had listened to my gut instinct and kept on drivin' when you begged me to stop at that convenience store to get somethin' to eat," Lenny said. "Guess I'm nothin' but a softie." The flashlight beam slipped a couple of inches, so it wasn't directly in Earl's eyes. "And while I sure as shit don't think that guy deserved to have his head blowed off, even if he *did* call you a hippie . . . man, doing that girl was wrong, Earl. Just plain wrong."

Lenny's mind replayed the scene at the convenience store. He is casually checking out the display of Little Debbie snacks when there's a thunderous blast and he's splattered with the clerk's blood. Behind him, Earl is holding the smoking magnum, his head and chest covered with more than just blood. Suddenly, a teenage girl who is standing by the soda cooler starts screaming. Earl walks over calmly, like he was going to ask her for her phone number, puts the gun against her head and blasts the back half clean off.

"Just plain wrong," Lenny said again, shaking his head. "Man, I begged you to just stay in the car and watch the money. And you carrying that fuckin' cannon around everywhere was just trouble waitin' to happen."

Earl's mouth opened to speak, but he closed it quickly.

"So now, instead of me bein' able to relax in some nice, fancy hotel somewhere, I gotta hide out in this smelly-ass shithole with the dumbest, ugliest, most annoying retard that ain't got the common sense God gave a rock . . ."

Earl brought the handgun around so fast that Lenny didn't have time to react. The first bullet hit Lenny in the throat. At once, his mouth filled with the hot, coppery taste of blood. Earl fired a second shot immediately, striking Lenny's chest. As Lenny fell backward, his finger contracted and the shotgun fired, the discharge lighting up the room with its brief brilliance. The blast sent Earl's lower jaw splintering across the cabin. Earl dropped his pistol, his hands flying to what was left of his face. Lenny fell straight backward, his head thumping onto one of the bags of cash, where it came to rest. He sputtered and choked but couldn't clear the blood filling his throat. His eyes followed Earl, who was dancing around the room making a gurgling sound until he stumbled against the open door and collapsed, falling to one side, his eyes open and staring directly at Lenny.

A cold, tingling sensation moved up from Lenny's toes. He knew he should try to stand, but he was too weak and too tired, so he just lay on the floor, looking over at Earl's dead, gloriously silent half-face, and grinned.

There was a slight scratching noise across the room. Lenny turned slowly to see the rat sitting next to the hole in the floor. He and the rat stared at each other for a long time until, eventually, the rat inched across the floor, crawled over Lenny's body to a box of Little Debbie Cupcakes and began gnawing.

S

A sharp wind cuts across the rooftop, pressing my father's cape flat against his back. He is standing on top of the short, narrow wall that rings our apartment building's roof. He teeters in the gust and I take a quick step toward him, but he holds out his hand to stop me. For twenty minutes, I have been trying to get him to climb down from the ledge, to give up his suicide plan. Another blast of wind raises goose bumps on my bare arms.

When my father turns from me to look down, I use the moment to steal another step closer to him. I have managed to close the gap to no more than fifteen feet. My best hope is to keep my father talking.

"Any people down there?" I ask.

My father lifts his head but doesn't turn toward me. He stares straight ahead, at a thick, pear-shaped cloud moving steadily across the sky. "No, thank God," he says. "I wouldn't want to hurt anyone else."

It takes me a minute to realize he's not referring to himself, but to my mother. He does turn then, and I can see how ridiculous he looks in that Superman getup of his. A flash of anger races through me at how embarrassing this will be for me if he goes through with the jump. But this is quickly replaced by the shame of having such a thought. Mostly, though, my eyes fix on that giant S stretched tight across his chest, the color of fresh blood, and it mutely screams the recent, drug-hazed words from my father's hospital bed that he says he never really meant and which I mostly believe. "See? See what you've done? If only you had come with us like we'd asked."

I sneak another step. "Shit, Dad, it was just an accident. Tragic, yes, but together we can get past it. Now *please* come down. You've got to stop trying to assign blame."

"Why not? There is always blame," my father says. "I was the one driving. I was the one looking down. I was the one who didn't steer away from the truck in time. Goddammit, I was the one who should've died! We've been through this a million times, Garrett. How many doctors have said I shouldn't be alive? That I must be superhuman to have survived?" He swivels to face me, extending his arms so I can see fully the Superman costume. Superman, gray-haired with a beer belly. "Well, here I am. And if I *am* a Superman, then I can't get hurt, right?"

He moves so fast I cannot react. In one motion he turns and steps off the roof. I run to the edge and lean over. I catch sight just as my father hits the sidewalk. He lands on his back. Our apartment building is ten stories high and he seems so small, yet I make out the widening halo of blood around his head, which is bent away so that I can't see his face. The only thing I do see clearly is that large red S on his chest. I am unable to move, to remove my eyes from it and I don't know how long I stay there, leaning over the roof, staring at that S, screaming, before unknown hands pull me away.

CALVIN BODENHEIMER
AND THE DALRYMPLE BULL

Each Saturday during the summer months, after his chores were done, and his mama had released him until suppertime, Calvin Bodenheimer headed into the woods that clothed the mountains behind his family's property. Sometimes he'd go with his best friend, Pete, but most often he'd follow the well-worn trails through the pines and oaks and hackberries by himself. There was a comforting isolation in the woods, yet Calvin never felt alone. At an early age, he developed a love for the birds, bugs, and mammals that lived in the forest, and he spent hours watching or trailing them.

For his twelfth birthday, his father presented Calvin with his first rifle. It was a big deal and, even though he'd already learned to shoot his father's rifle, and had done so many times, being trusted with one of his own was a defining moment in the boy's life.

The first weekend after he'd gotten the gun, Calvin hurried across the pasture behind the house, disappearing up the dirt path at the edge of the woods. He felt taller, somehow, as he walked along hefting the rifle in his hand. After a half hour of hiking, Calvin took a familiar path that led from the main trail down to a wide creek. He'd been here many times—it was one of his favorite spots—and he sat down in the V formed by the large, projecting roots of a yellow birch that grew on the edge of the creek's bank. Calvin unlaced his boots and stowed them in a cavity that had formed beneath the undercut base of the tree. He plucked a blade of grass and wedged it between two front teeth. Calvin leaned back then and closed his eyes, grateful for the birch's cool shade on one of the year's hottest days.

A splash drew Calvin's attention to his left. Fifty yards away, he spotted a dark brown wedge gliding across Cone Creek. He spit out the blade of grass and sat up. His eyes fixed on the beaver moving in a lazy arc, leaving a long wake across the water. Calvin's hand swept the ground next to his leg until it met the sun-warmed metal of his rifle's barrel. The bright sun reflected off the water's surface, making it hard for the boy to draw a clear bead on the approaching animal.

The beaver changed course and veered toward Calvin. The animal swam into a shady section of water just beneath where the boy sat. Calvin lined his sight directly at a point between the beaver's eyes. Trembling, he tracked the animal's path, keeping aim. The finger on the trigger tensed slightly, but, at the last moment, Calvin lowered the barrel and watched the beaver swim a short way down from where he rested before clambering up the muddy bank and disappearing into the brush.

Calvin never brought the weapon into the woods again. He preferred to keep it at home where he would shoot only at cans he'd set atop the fence post, or at apples growing on the tree at the far end of the pasture.

Dreama Dalrymple was sixteen in 1941, the year the Japanese bombed Pearl Harbor. Her father, Ezra, operated the largest dairy farm in Mitchell County, North Carolina, with the help of his only son, George, and three hired hands. The day after Christmas, following a heated argument with his father, George Dalrymple strode off the family farm with nothing more than two shirts and one pair of patched pants rolled into a duffle, which he slung over his shoulder. George was headed for Raleigh to enlist in the navy, just as boys all over the country were doing that fateful December.

Having lost her mother that spring to pneumonia, Dreama was terrified about the prospect of losing her brother, too. After George's departure, Dreama watched her father, weakened from chronic heart problems, struggle to maintain the farm (one of the hired men having followed her brother into the service). She helped as much as she could while still going to high school, offering more than once to drop out. Her father was adamant she stay in school, telling his daughter that her mother always dreamed of her children going to college and getting what she had called "a real job."

It was during that difficult and joyless spring of 1942 that Calvin Bodenheimer, a freshman at Mitchell High, noticed the pretty but sad farmer's daughter in the class ahead of him. Shy by nature, he never considered approaching Dreama Dalrymple. But their school was small, with no more than 350 students in all, so it was easy for Calvin to position himself near her in the cafeteria, or at Friday assemblies. He'd sit where he could pretend to read and then glance over the top of his book to steal a glimpse of Dreama's dark hair, which fell in natural waves to her shoulders, perfectly framing the smooth, pale skin of her face. But it was her eyes, green like spring grass, which captivated Calvin the most.

He confided his feelings for Dreama to only one person—his best friend, Pete Shockley, who was the son of one of Ezra Dalrymple's farm hands. Proving the old saw that opposites attract, Pete was as outgoing as Calvin was bashful. Each day at school, Pete watched his friend mooning over Dreama and tried to get to him to approach her and, at the very least, say hello. Frustrated by Calvin's timid reticence, it was only Pete's loyalty to his buddy that kept him from going up to Dreama and telling her about Calvin's crush.

So as the nation entangled itself in war overseas, one teenager in Mitchell County, North Carolina, set upon himself the mission of bringing together a quarryman's son and the farmer's daughter.

Spring calving is one of the busiest times on a dairy farm. In addition to the regular milking chores, calves have to be separated and bottle-fed, bull calves evaluated for their meat potential and culled as needed, heifers cared for as future milkers themselves. For Dreama Dalrymple, that meant on schooldays helping her father an hour or more each morning before walking nearly a mile down the dusty, winding road from their farm to the state-maintained route where she'd wait for the school bus. After school, too, there was no time for extracurricular activities. She would ride home following the dismissal bell and work until it was time to make supper. Following the meal, her father would clean up the kitchen while she studied and did her homework.

Between classes on the Friday during the last week of April, Pete and Calvin stood in the hallway at Mitchell High reading a poster announcing May Frolic, the annual school dance, which was to take place in two weeks.

"This is your chance," Pete said, jabbing Calvin in the arm with his elbow. "All the girls wait to be asked to May Frolic. You have *got* to ask Dreama."

"No chance. Besides, she's probably already been asked by somebody else." Calvin stared at the poster a long time. "Anyway, she doesn't know me from Adam. How would it look if somebody she's never so much as said hey to came up and asked her to the dance?"

"I'm guessing it would look like he liked her, you moron."

"Don't call me moron, moron." Calvin started walking down the hall. "So who are you going to ask?"

"Remember that girl in my algebra class I told you about? Ruby Katherine?"

"The one who snorts when she laughs?"

"Yeah, that's her."

"I thought you said you couldn't stand it when she snorted, that it made your head hurt."

"Well, she's pretty. I'll just make sure not to tell any jokes."

Calvin laughed and shoved Pete against the lockers.

"So are you going to ask Dreama, or not?" Pete asked.

"I guess not. It'd be different if she at least knew I existed."

"Then I suppose we got to get you noticed, my friend."

"How?"

"I don't know yet," Pete said. "But give me time."

Calvin didn't have to wait long for his friend's plan. Three days later, he was sitting on a shaded patch of new-mown grass beneath one of two large chestnut oaks that grew on the wide stretch of lawn outside the high school's cafeteria. He was eating a bologna sandwich and vainly attempting to decipher the cryptic language of *Romeo and Juliet*, on which he was to be tested the next day. A large shadow fell across the book.

"Here you are," Pete said, dropping his own books on the grass and sitting down beside Calvin. "Whatchya eating there?"

"Bologna."

"Ugh. I think I'll just keep my liver mush."

Pete unwrapped wax paper from around a thick sandwich and took an enormous bite, a glob of mustard squeezing onto his finger. Calvin finished the last of his own sandwich and took a Granny Smith apple from his lunch sack for dessert.

After Pete swallowed, he licked the mustard from his hand. "I bet you didn't ask Dreama to May Frolic yet, did you?"

Calvin looked up from his book, making no effort to hide his exasperation. He shook his head and turned back to his reading.

"Well, I think I know how you can not only get Dreama Dalrymple's attention, but really impress her in the process."

"How?"

"Pa works at the Dalrymples' dairy."

"I know. So?" Calvin's breaths quickened. He hoped Pete didn't notice.

"So, shut up and listen and I'll tell you."

"I'm listening."

"We were sitting around the supper table after church yesterday and Pa starts to tell this funny story about something that happened on the farm that morning. I'm not really paying much attention until I hear him mention Dreama's name."

Pete stopped talking and took a bite of the liver mush sandwich. He chewed slowly. Calvin knew Pete was trying to get his goat and fought the urge to react. After what seemed an eternity to Calvin, his friend swallowed, and then wiped the corners of his mouth with a pinky.

"Now, where was I? Oh, yes, I remember. So, Pa goes on about this young farmhand that Mr. Dalrymple just hired on account of their being short because of the war and all. It turns out this new guy is Walter Jennings."

"*The* Walter Jennings? Who lost his eye playing linebacker here a couple years back?"

"Yep, one and the same. Anyway, seems Walter tried to enlist in the Marines right after Pearl Harbor, but was rejected because of his eye. So he comes back home and starts looking for a job, and since ol' man Dalrymple is short a couple fellas, he takes on Walter straight away. Now, here's the kicker, Cal. Walter's only been working on the farm a few months, but it's become obvious to everyone that he's smitten, as my Pa says, with Dreama. You can imagine my interest in this story perked right up at that point."

Calvin lifted the apple to his mouth, but realized he'd lost his appetite and laid it on the grass.

"Pa says all the men started teasing Walter pretty good and egging him on to talk to Dreama each time she'd come out to help with the chores, but it seems ol' Walter's about got you beat in the shyness department, my friend. So, one day one of the guys gets this idea, and the idea is Tiny."

"He has a small idea? What the heck's that supposed to mean?" Calvin asked.

"Not a tiny *idea*, shit-for-brains. Tiny is the name of Mr. Dalrymple's Holstein bull. But the name is what you'd call ironic, seeing as Tiny is about the biggest, meanest bull in all of North Carolina. Hell, even my Pa is afraid of that animal, and that's saying something."

"So how's Tiny supposed to get Walter in good with Dreama?"

"I'll tell you," Pete said, "but I've come to think more like it's *your* way to get in good with her, Cal."

"How?"

Pete tossed the last bite of the liver mush sandwich into his mouth and grinned. He went on to explain that Tiny, according to his father, was left pretty much alone for most of the year, until breeding season. He was Mr. Dalrymple's favorite and most reliable stud, but when it came time to move Tiny to the breeding pen, Dreama's father was the only person who could even approach the bull. And even he was wary, having been gored in the thigh several years back. So with the passage of time, Tiny's reputation for orneriness and foul temper (not entirely undeserved) had grown among those who worked at the dairy. It had become a common threat to toss any slackers or laggards into the pasture with Tiny.

Dreama, for her part, was a hard worker who prided herself on being able to keep up with the men on the farm. If one of the hands implied she was incapable of doing a particular chore because she was a girl, and offered to do it for her, she'd been known to fix that man with the coldest of stares, and then redouble her efforts to the task. While there were certainly physical limitations at times, she managed, for the most part, to pull her weight. And should one of the men make the mistake of pointing out those limitations, she was apt to reiterate her frequent challenge to that man. Namely, she would say, if any hand wanted to show her that he was a real man, then all he had to do was tie a ribbon around one of Tiny's massive horns. As a joke, she'd even placed a pink ribbon on a nail inside the milking parlor for just such a purpose. It became the source of teasing among the men, who never considered the challenge seriously.

After finishing his story, Pete leaned back on the grass, propping himself on both elbows. Both boys remained quiet for a few minutes before Calvin spoke.

"So what you're saying is that I should get myself killed trying to tie that ribbon on Tiny's horn?"

"Calvin, my boy, you are a damned genius."

"Do I look crazy?"

"Well, you're in love, and I can't rightly see there's a whole lot of difference." Pete sat up. "Thing is, Cal, you'd better make a decision quick, 'cause I suspect ol' Walter is likely to try it himself."

"Uh uh, no way," Calvin said.

"Suit yourself. I guess Dreama and Walter'll make a handsome couple, at that." Pete folded the paper bag from his lunch and tucked it under the front cover of his math text. He gathered his books and stood up. "Gotta go. I got algebra, and Mrs. Crowder don't take kindly to tardiness. See you on the bus?"

"Yeah."

That would likely have been the end of any consideration Calvin was to give Pete's foolhardy suggestion had he not happened to pass Dreama and her best friend, Connie Sills, as he made his way to biology. The girls were standing next to Connie's open locker, talking. As he passed them, Calvin heard the words "May Frolic" and felt his face flush. On impulse, he stopped at the water fountain attached to the wall a few feet away. He leaned slightly toward the girls, trying to hear more.

". . . *have* to go," Connie said, grabbing Dreama's arm and shaking it. "Don't be stupid, Dreama. This is the best dance of the year."

"I just can't decide," Dreama said. "Besides, who would I go with?"

There was a sudden push against Calvin's shoulder, causing water to shoot against his neck and soak the front of his shirt.

"You gonna drink the fountain dry, or let someone else have some?"

Calvin stood, wiping the water from his neck, and turned to see Artie Landrum, the football team's center. Calvin glanced over and saw Dreama and Connie watching them and felt heat rise in his face. He hurried down the hall, Artie already forgotten, and Dreama's last words repeating in his mind. By the end of biology, Calvin had convinced himself what he needed to do.

Light shone from the main window of the Dalrymple farmhouse at nine-thirty the following Saturday evening when Calvin and Pete crept past the pine board fence that lined the front of the property. The earthy-sweet scent of cow manure was thick in the warm spring air. A crescent moon did little to illumine the night. The boys followed the fence until the dark shape of the milking parlor was visible about a hundred yards beyond the house. They climbed over and could hear the soft snorts of cows a short distance from them in the pasture. Calvin stepped in a large, soft mound of manure, glad that Pete had had the forethought to borrow without his father's knowledge a couple pairs of his Tingleys. He stopped to shake the manure off the rubber boot and Pete ran into him.

"Hey!" Pete said, whispering. "Give me some warning next time."

Calvin nodded and stepped carefully the remainder of the way to the barn. The main door was open, and when the two teens went in, the air was heavy and still and about ten degrees warmer than outdoors. Their presence caused the calves, who were in a row of pens lining the near side of the building, to begin moving around and calling to be fed. Pete clicked on a flashlight he'd brought. The light caused the calves to become more excited and beckon for their bottles.

"They're making a hell of a racket," Pete said. "They keep it up and Mr. Dalrymple'll hear it and come out to see what the fuss is about."

"Then let's find that stupid ribbon and get out of here," Calvin said.

Pete shone the flashlight around the barn as Calvin stood at the door, watching the house. A shadow moved across the window and Calvin wondered if it was Dreama or her father. His mind conjured an image of Dreama in her nightgown. A tap on his shoulder startled him.

"Jesus Christ, don't sneak up on me like that."

His anger vanished upon seeing Pete standing behind him, his right arm extended with a long, dirt-smudged ribbon dangling from his hand. Immediately, Calvin was flooded with fear at the realization of what he was supposed to do with the ribbon.

"Time to find Tiny," Pete said, clicking off the flashlight and walking out the door.

"I don't know about this." Calvin hadn't moved. The calves continued to cry to be fed, banging and kicking against the slats of their pens.

"Do you want a date with Dreama, or not?"

"Yeah, but this is stupid. I'm gonna get killed."

"No, you won't. Tiny's probably sleeping. If you're quiet enough you can sneak up, tie the ribbon and get out without him ever even knowing."

"Yeah, right," Calvin said.

"Now come on, before you lose your nerve completely."

Without waiting for a response, Pete disappeared around the front of the barn and Calvin hurried to catch up. From previous visits with his father, Pete knew that Tiny stayed by himself in a small, fenced pasture next to some woods at the far end of the farm. They followed the thin beam of the flashlight as it traced the angles and bends of the fence line. When they reached the near end of Tiny's field, Pete held up his hand to stop Calvin.

They looked between the two topmost boards. Neither boy could see anything in the blackness. There was no sound from the pasture. Calvin was trembling and his breaths came rapidly.

"Here," Pete said, handing the ribbon to Calvin, who took it reluctantly.

Pete moved the light in a slow, horizontal pattern across the field. When he'd reach one end, he'd advance the light a bit and move it back across in the opposite direction. He'd made several passes with no sign of the bull.

"Let's go," Calvin said. "He's not here. They must have moved him somewhere else. If he was here, we'd hear him, don't you think?"

"I suppose so. Let's just keep . . ."

Just then, the light landed on the bull, who was lying down, asleep. Pete inched the beam across the animal's bulky body. Framed in absolute darkness, Tiny seemed even more enormous than in the daylight. The bull's eyes were closed. Pete trailed the light's beam along Tiny's massive left horn, pausing involuntarily on the pointed end before turning it off.

"Uh, Calvin . . . I'm thinking we'd better forget this, after all."

Calvin's heart beat so rapidly it felt like a small bird was trapped in his chest. He lifted his hand and opened it so that the ribbon draped across his palm. There was a dark, wet sweat stain in the middle where he'd gripped it. He looked out toward the indistinct form of the sleeping bull. Pete was right, and he knew it. Calvin checked back over his shoulder at the Dalrymples' house. There were no lights on now. He imagined Dreama alone in her bedroom, asleep and dreaming, and then turned back to his friend.

"Keep the light just in front of me at all times," Calvin said, stepping one foot on the lowest board of the fence. "And no matter what happens, don't you come in this field with Tiny. Just run and get help if I need it. You hear?"

Pete was too stunned to answer. He nodded and reached up to put his hand on Calvin's shoulder, squeezing quick and hard. He turned the flashlight back on, and as soon as Calvin dropped to the other side, he pointed it on the ground to lead him. Calvin didn't have anything remotely like a plan, and as he moved as quietly as possible across the pasture, he thought that, perhaps, that was for the best. Instinct might be his only chance in this foolish endeavor.

Calvin could smell the bull before he could see him. It was a heavy, musky masculine odor that carried the unmistakable air of danger. Calvin stopped for a moment and lifted the ribbon close to his face, twisting a large, drooping loop, and for a moment he was stunned by the unreality of what he was attempting. Had he been able to breathe, he might have laughed. But any laugh he might have considered was stifled by the abrupt snorting sound in front of him. Through the circle of ribbon still held before his eyes, Calvin saw the dark shape of Tiny shifting. He watched, unblinking and holding his breath, until the bull settled and the movement stopped. The free ends of the ribbon vibrated as they hung from his hands.

Calvin took just one more step when Tiny swung his massive head toward him. Calvin froze, his arm still straight out with the ribbon dangling, looking like a poor imitation of a bullfighter. With surprising speed, the bull stood and turned. Tiny grunted, and it was the unexpected loudness of it that spurred Calvin to run. In the darkness, the only thing visible was the bright circle of Pete's flashlight. Calvin headed straight for it and was only vaguely aware of the sound of his friend's screaming at him to run faster.

About ten feet from the fence, Calvin felt the impact against the back of his legs. Had he been just a foot closer, his head would have been driven directly into the top board of the fence, but Tiny had tossed his head when he hit Calvin, sending him airborne, just clearing the top of the fence, to land on his left side with an audible crack.

There was a loud ringing in his ears, so Calvin could not make out the muffled words that Pete was shouting down at him. Calvin let his head roll toward the field. The light from his fallen flashlight caught the ring in Tiny's nose and despite the sharp pain radiating up from his fractured leg, he smiled as he watched the bull jerking his head back and forth in an attempt to shake off the ribbon that swung from the end of his left horn.

And the last thing he remembered before passing out was Ezra Dalrymple and Dreama running up to where he lay, and the look of utter concern on Dreama's face.

One frigid Saturday evening in January in 1975, Calvin Bodenheimer was sitting in the Recovery Room Lounge off Route 164, finishing his fourth Pabst Blue Ribbon, contemplating a fifth. A few other men, regulars like Calvin—the mill foreman, one of the linemen from the electric company, a retired postal worker—were leaning on the bar, nursing their own drinks. They all took turns spinning tales of bravado from their youth.

Calvin listened to Norbie, the mill foreman, roll out the story of how he'd wrestled a black bear in the Yancey County Fair back in 1936 to win three dollars. Calvin sipped his beer, smiling and nodding at appropriate points. Norbie concluded, as always, by lifting his shirt to expose the thick, long scar that ran across his rib cage.

"That bear," Norbie said, "had a wide leather strap tied around her muzzle, and they was supposed to file her claws, but the handler was a two-bit drunk who forgot, and I'll be damned if she didn't hook the sharp end of one of them nails into my flesh. If I hadn't rolled off when I did, I woulda been lying there with my guts strewn from one side of that dirt pit t'other, that sow suckin' them down like they was spaghetti."

The men at the bar grinned and nodded together, silently acknowledging the good fortune of their friend. Calvin drained his glass and waggled it toward Ted, the bartender, a lanky man with leathery skin and wild, bushy eyebrows. Ted refilled Calvin's glass and slid it back.

"You know, Cal," Ted said, "Norbie's bear story reminds me of that thing with you and old man Dalrymple's bull. You fellas remember that one?"

Calvin, who'd just been thinking about the bull himself, looked down the bar at each of the men nodding their heads, and then gulped down two-thirds of his beer. "It ain't such a great story."

"The hell it ain't," Ted said. He knit his brow and pursed his lips. "Shitfire, what the heck was the name of that girl, Calvin?"

Calvin stared into his glass, watching tiny bubbles burst silently around the circle where the beer met the glass.

"Dreama Dalrymple," he said.

"Right. How could I forget a name like that? What happened to her, anyways?"

Calvin was silent, still staring down into the beer glass, but he sensed the other men watching him, waiting for his answer. Of course, there was no answer.

"Don't know," he said. "Not long after, she moved away."

"I remember," Dixon, the electric company lineman, who was a tad slow, said. "You almost got yourself killed so she'd go to some dance or something with you. Ain't that right?"

Calvin looked down the bar and smiled. "Well, it's kinda hard to dance with a leg that's broke in three places."

"But you did date her soon after, right?" Ted asked.

"Yes, twice. She moved less than three months after my stupid stunt with Tiny."

Turning back to the bar and staring down into his beer glass, Calvin unsuccessfully fought the bittersweet memory of his brief romance with Dreama Dalrymple. While all their friends danced at the May Frolic, Calvin and Dreama went instead to dinner at Sissy's, a diner that used to sit on a once-busy section of 226 just outside Bakersville. They ate fried egg and tomato sandwiches and drank Coke and shared a banana split for dessert. Dreama did most of the talking and, although he'd been nervous when she drove up to his house to pick him up, she managed to make him feel at ease by the time they'd gotten to Sissy's. They stayed at the restaurant until Sissy kicked them out at eight-thirty so she could close up. After leaving the diner, Dreama

drove them to a cleared spot by Cone Creek, where they sat in
the truck and talked until she had to get home at ten-thirty. She
asked him questions about his family, about his likes and dislikes,
what he wanted to do with his life. And there, leaning against
the passenger door of Ezra Dalrymple's '37 Ford truck, Calvin
Bodenheimer fell in love for the only time in his life.

Although they hung around together at school from that
point on, Calvin and Dreama only went on one more date, to
an end-of-year party in the school gym during the third week
of June. Two days later, a gray-blue car belonging to the U.S.
Navy drove down the dust and gravel drive to the Dalrymples'
farmhouse, where two uniformed sailors told Ezra and Dreama
that George had died in the Pacific when his carrier was attacked
by Japanese Zeros. The shock of the news caused Mr. Dalrymple
to have a heart attack from which he never fully recovered.
Dreama was sent down the mountain, to Shelby, to live with
her mother's sister's family. Calvin saw her only one more time,
a few weeks later, when she came with her aunt to move Ezra
from the hospital in Spruce Pine to Shelby. She told her aunt
she was going to see Connie, but instead drove to Calvin's house.
She promised to call him often and, before leaving, kissed him
and hugged him hard.

Seven months after telling his story to his friends at the Recovery
Room, Calvin was sitting on the front porch of his house, reading
the Sunday newspaper. At seven-thirty in the morning, the day
was already hot, but clear. From where he sat, Calvin had an
unobstructed view of Roan Mountain in the west. It would be
a good day, he thought, to hike into the woods and sit in the
crook of his favorite birch tree, the one he'd discovered as a
boy, and drop his line into Cone Creek.

When he was finished with the front section of the paper,
Calvin took a sip of coffee and picked up the local news. Most
folks chose to read the "big" papers out of Charlotte or
Asheville, but he still preferred to read the *Mitchell News-Journal*.

Skipping the usual stories about urban encroachment versus county development that dominated the front page, Calvin instead read, with amusement, an article detailing two local women's demand that the management of the stone quarry, where Calvin worked as a plug-and-feather driller, provide equal pay for its female employees. On the back page of the local section were listed the obituaries. Having reached fifty, Calvin had developed the habit of checking the list of the recently deceased for any acquaintances. When he saw the name Ezra Dalrymple, he sat up and adjusted his reading glasses.

Ezra's obituary indicated that he had died in Shelby two days earlier, at the age of seventy-eight. However, his funeral and burial were planned for ten o'clock the next morning at the Sweet Creek Cemetery near Bakersville, where, after nearly thirty-five years, Ezra was to rejoin his wife.

Calvin dropped the newspaper onto the porch and rocked back, staring off toward the green swell of Roan Mountain, but not really seeing it. Indistinct images of faces from his past, as if he were looking at them through water, swirled in his memory. There was Tiny's, enormous and black-and-white, with dark, surprisingly intelligent eyes; Ezra Dalrymple's, red and straining as he struggled, with Pete, to carry Calvin from the house to the truck in order to drive him to the doctor; his father's, a sun-hardened quarryman's face with its odd mix of fear and anger after he'd met them at the hospital. But the face Calvin most remembered was Dreama's.

Following breakfast on Monday, Calvin dressed in the navy suit he'd laid out the night before. It was snug across the shoulders and although he could button it, the jacket strained against his midsection, so he decided to leave it unbuttoned. It had been some time since he'd had occasion to wear a suit.

It was a twenty-minute drive to the cemetery from his house. Despite running the air conditioner on high, by the time Calvin pulled through the wrought iron arch at its entrance at five minutes after ten, his hands were sweating. From the parking lot he could see a small group of people gathered in the middle of a field of headstones to his left. He brushed the sleeves of his jacket and walked toward the group.

There were no more than ten people clustered next to the gravesite. A few turned toward Calvin when he approached. He stood at the near end, opposite the preacher, who was extolling Ezra Dalrymple's virtues, assuring those present that he was now safely nestled in the arms of the Lord. Calvin had no difficulty recognizing Dreama, who stood next to the preacher with her arm around the shoulders of a young man of about twenty, who looked to Calvin to be a younger version of Ezra himself. Despite the obvious fatigue of the recent days, Dreama appeared to have aged well. While no longer pretty in the girlish way Calvin remembered from high school, she had grown into a strikingly handsome woman.

When the brief service ended, Calvin waited at the end of the line of friends and family, who took turns offering their condolences to Dreama. When it was his turn, Calvin stepped forward, secretly wiping his palms on the back of his pants.

"Hello, Dreama," he said. "You won't remember me, but we knew each other in high school."

Her smile was immediate and wide. "My God. Calvin Bodenheimer. You haven't changed one little bit."

Dreama stepped toward him and they embraced.

"I'm so sorry about your father," Calvin said when they stepped apart. "He was one of the most decent men I've ever known."

"Thank you, Calvin. You're so sweet to come. But he'd not been well for a long time. I hate to say it, but it's really a blessing in many ways."

Calvin nodded and had the urge to wipe his hands again, but resisted.

"I'd like you to meet my son," Dreama said, turning to the young man beside her. "Calvin Bodenheimer, this is my son, Evan Orr. Evan, this is the sweetest and craziest man I ever knew."

The two men shook hands.

"Evan, do you remember the story of the boy who tied a ribbon on your grandfather's bull to impress me?"

"How could I not," Evan said. "You've told me that story only about a million times."

Calvin felt warmth in his cheeks.

"Well, can you blame me?" Dreama said. "No one, before or since, has ever done such a brave, if stupid, thing for me. That's not the kind of thing a girl forgets."

"Stupid is the key word there, Evan," Calvin said. "Your mother and grandfather saved my life that night."

"Nonsense. If I'm not mistaken, you only broke your leg," Dreama said.

Calvin smiled, not at being caught at his false dramatics, but at the fact that after so many years, the details of that night had stayed with Dreama.

"Mom, I'm going to go wait in the car," Evan said. "It was nice to meet you, sir. I actually thought my mother made up that story about the bull."

"My pleasure, too, Evan."

Calvin watched him walk down the row of graves to the drive and turn toward a group of relatives standing together in the parking lot. When Calvin looked back at Dreama, she was staring at her father's casket.

"Where did time go, Calvin?" she asked. "I didn't realize how much I missed Mitchell County until we drove up yesterday. It's so beautiful here. And you know what's funny? Even though I've lived most of my life elsewhere, I still think of this as home."

Calvin followed her gaze past the fence of the cemetery, where the hazy outline of the Blue Ridge Mountains lined the horizon. He nodded, knowing the truth she had spoken, and the reason he'd never followed her all those years ago.

Dreama went to the casket and bent to kiss it. When she turned back, she took Calvin's arm in hers and led him away.

"So, tell me about your life, Calvin. Are you married? Children?"

"No and no," he said. "I've come close, I guess, more than once, but it just never worked out." He looked at her. "How about you? Is your husband here?"

"Evan's father and I divorced about five years ago. And to tell the truth, it probably should've been long before that, but Evan was in high school and I tried to stick it out, thinking it was better for him, but . . ."

They reached the paved drive and turned for the short walk to the cars.

"So are you headed back to Shelby?" Calvin asked. He was aware his heart rate had crept up.

"Actually, we live in Charlotte. I'm a city girl now."

"City life has its advantages. And Charlotte's a pretty decent city, if you have to live in one."

"You'll have to come visit, Calvin. Do you like baseball? Evan has a friend who works for the Knights. He can get tickets."

"That sounds fine," Calvin said. "I'd like that."

"Great." Dreama squeezed his arm, giving it a slight tug.

They'd reached the parking area and Evan stood holding open the passenger door of their car.

"Thank you again for coming today," Dreama said. "I'll call you."

"That'd be just fine, Dreama."

Dreama kissed Calvin on the cheek and climbed into the sedan. Evan and Calvin shook hands once more and Calvin stepped back, watching until their car left the cemetery and vanished down the hill that leads toward Bakersville and the Interstate.

Calvin loosened the knot of his tie and took off his jacket. He looked up at the cloudless sky and knew it was likely to hit well above ninety degrees by mid-afternoon. And down in the quarry it'd be ten degrees hotter, but he'd been a stone driller for over thirty years and heat was part of the deal. He checked his watch. By the time he got home, changed into his work clothes, and drove to the quarry, lunch shift would just about be ending. He could get in plenty of work in the afternoon. But Calvin decided instead to take his fishing rod and head to Cone Creek, to sit at the base of his favorite birch tree, as he had for forty plus years. There, he was always able to put things in perspective while doing nothing more than watching the unhurried water slide past. With any luck, he thought, he might even spot a beaver.

On the drive home, Calvin thought about Dreama's last words, how she had vowed to call him. He allowed his mind to play the fantasy of their getting together again and finding something they'd both longed for over these many years. It was a gratifying thought and it made him smile. But he knew better. As she said, she was a city girl now. And he'd never be anything but a cutter, as much a part of the mountains as the stone he split each day. Besides, he reminded himself, despite her promise, she hadn't even asked for his phone number.

He laughed at that thought as he steered his pickup through the winding curves of Mitchell County. And there was no sadness, no regret, hiding in his laugh. For Calvin Bodenheimer knew that the real tests in life are not random, but rather the ones we give ourselves, and that long ago, he had taken the test that would define his life from that moment on. And he had passed.

CITYSCAPE

1

One of the great charms of the mid-sized southern city in which I live is the hodgepodge of neighborhoods that fill its borders, each unique and reflective of the people who live in them. One of the oldest, and largest, is an irregular grid of streets filled with closely packed, single-family houses. This neighborhood bridges two large medical centers, and is home to a diverse group of doctors, teachers, students and other upwardly mobile types, as well as working-class families. For decades, it enjoyed a reputation as a friendly, almost quaint neighborhood, well-known for lazy summer evenings idled away in front porch gatherings, and temperate autumns when small children run and play up and down the sidewalks.

Several years ago, during the week after Thanksgiving, a newly arrived family decorated their house for Christmas. The display was enormous and elaborate, with every bush and tree adjacent to the home ablaze with hundreds of colorful bulbs. The house, too, was framed with blinking lights. But the centerpiece of the holiday display was an enormous nativity scene set up across the front lawn. The figures of the crèche were life-sized and included the three Magi and several animals. The owners had also carefully wired an angel to the eave so it hung suspended above the scene, as large as any of the figures below it, its wings and arms spread wide. The angel was positioned below a large, illuminated star fastened atop the roof.

The display quickly became the talk of the neighborhood and even found itself the subject of stories in the newspaper and on the local TV news. Following the appearance of these stories, people from all over the city, county, and beyond began driving by to witness it, necessitating that the family keep the display lit up later and later each night to accommodate the viewers.

But as it turned out, the great, bright star that shone down on the holy scene was situated on the roof such that it was exactly even with the window to the neighbor's master bedroom. So bright was this star that, even with the blinds closed, its brightness punched through enough to light the room as though it were midday. The couple who lived in this neighboring house, a middle-aged insurance executive and his wife, explained the problem to the newcomers, making it clear that they weren't angry, certain that the people with the ornate decorations would be embarrassed when they learned of their unintended rudeness.

It turned out the new arrivals were devout fundamentalists who informed the sleepless couple that, while they might be sorry for the inconvenience they were causing, they'd come to the conclusion, through prayerful consideration, that God had chosen them to inspire others to find the true, but sadly lost, meaning of Christmas. They pointed to the growing stream of visitors each night as evidence that this was right. So rather than politely turning off the offending star at a reasonable hour each evening, it stayed on all night, every night the following week. The police were called out, but they had no better success at convincing the owners of the display to cooperate. Lawsuits were threatened, but the insurance executive and his wife knew that it would take weeks or months for the courts to settle the issue, and by then, the lights would have been taken down and the point moot.

The newspaper reporter who'd written the original piece about the decorations was alerted to the feud, and the story quickly became the most talked-about issue in town, starting a citywide debate about religious rights, property rights, and common courtesy. Opinions, based on emotional letters to the editor, showed nearly even support for both neighbors.

Six days before Christmas, in the middle of the night, a loud popping noise awakened residents of several homes along the street where the controversy occurred. Someone, it turned out, had shot and destroyed the ersatz Star of Bethlehem. The insurance executive was immediately accused, but he denied it vehemently and no evidence was ever produced to link him to the shooting.

Despite this, two days later, when going outside to retrieve his morning paper, the executive discovered his Lexus sedan had four slashed tires and two shattered windows. Assuming it was the work of his neighbor, he stormed next door and demanded immediate restitution for the damage. The newcomer swore he'd no knowledge of the vandalism, but implied that whoever had, in fact, committed the act had certainly been sent by God to atone for the sacrilege the insurance executive himself had carried out. A shoving match ensued, but the men's wives were able to separate them.

The irate insurance man strode to the back of his own house, to the small, detached garage, and found a sledgehammer he'd used some time ago while building a fence. He marched back to the neighbor's front yard and proceeded to swing the tool at each of the parts of the nativity scene, demolishing the heavy, plaster figures one after another. The owners of the crèche came running out of their house, as did the insurance executive's wife, and together tried to stop the frenzied destruction. More struggling ensued, and only moments before the police arrived, the insurance executive managed to shove the other man to the ground. He lifted the sledgehammer and swung it backward in order to bring it down on the figure of the Christ child. Unfortunately, the neighbor's wife was standing right behind him and took the force of the hammer directly on the top of her head. Before the ambulance arrived, she was dead.

The insurance executive was arrested and charged with negligent homicide, but because of the mitigating circumstances and the fact that he lacked a prior criminal record, he was released on bail and sent home to await his trial. Two days later, on Christmas morning, distraught over causing the death of the woman and the shame he'd brought on his family, the insurance executive hung himself in his basement. His widow sold their house within three weeks, for far less than its value, and told none of her friends where she was moving. The executive's neighbor, beside himself with grief over his wife's death, would not leave his house after her funeral and left all of the shattered decorations and figures untouched on his lawn. Several months later, responding to complaints from the neighborhood association, the city cleaned it up and billed him for the service. Subsequent to the publicity of these tragedies, the persons who'd shot the star and vandalized the car came forward to confess their crimes.

The neighborhood has only recently returned to something close to its old ambiance, but now if you drive around that area at Christmastime, you will find a section, several blocks wide, where no one decorates their house for the holiday.

2

Some eight or nine years ago, a young man, the son of a prominent national politician, was attending the small, prestigious university in our city. One day, after driving around town and noticing a number of homeless persons, he decided he needed to do something to help these unfortunates who he felt had, as he'd later tell his roommate, slipped between the holes in society's safety net. Money, he decided, was too easy and too impersonal and too often misappropriated by those in charge of distributing it. He wanted to do something tangible.

When, after several weeks, he was unable to think of anything specific, it occurred to him that his problem stemmed from not having an adequate understanding of the circumstances in which these homeless people lived day after day. The solution seemed obvious. With spring break approaching, he backed out of an intended trip to Mexico with a group of friends and, instead, made plans to spend the entire week living on the streets of our city, subsisting only on what he received in donations from strangers, or what he could otherwise find. His roommate tried to talk him out of this noble but foolish scheme, sensibly explaining that his friend could ultimately do more for the downtrodden by lobbying his father, whom most expected to make a run for the Presidency in the next election, to endorse legislation that would improve the lot of the poor in general.

But the young man was undeterred. The final week of school before the break he stopped shaving and began wearing the same clothes each day. On the final day of classes, immediately following his last exam, he went back to his dorm, wrote a note to his roommate wishing him a good time in Mexico, then left campus.

Eight days later, on the evening before classes were to resume, the young man walked into his room at school, disheveled, dirty, and subdued. His roommate, anxious to hear about his friend's social experiment, pressed the young man for details of his week on the streets. The latter was reluctant to talk about it, explaining only that there was a vast subculture of homeless persons unknown to the majority of people who pass by them every day without a thought. He wouldn't go into specifics, but did mention that he had befriended a man whom he knew only as T, and that T had, in some way he wouldn't elaborate on, saved his life.

As the new semester began, the young man was unable to concentrate on his studies and skipped classes frequently, sometimes disappearing for hours on end, only to show up in the middle of the night. It wasn't long before he started to be gone for several days at a time. His grades suffered and he was soon at risk of failing. The roommate, concerned about his friend, called the young man's parents and explained what had occurred, and the personality changes that had taken place.

The following weekend, the politician and his wife came to the campus to see their son and to find out what was happening to him. He wasn't in his dorm room and no one knew where he was. They waited there until shortly after midnight, when at last the young man showed up. A loud argument ensued involving the young man, his father, and his roommate, which was witnessed by many students in the residence hall. There was some pushing and shoving and the young man threatened to kill his father if he didn't leave him alone. The campus police were called, but before they arrived, the young man walked out of the dormitory, ostensibly to cool off. To this day the young man has not been seen again.

A few days after the fight at school it became obvious that the young man wasn't coming back, so his father, using his considerable wealth and political clout, arranged for the FBI and private investigators to track him down. But even with these extensive resources, no trace of the young man was found. The homeless man known as T was identified and located. He was found wearing a sweatshirt that had belonged to the young man. T was taken into custody and questioned at length, but he was unable to provide any information that could help in determining where the young man had gone.

Months later, blaming himself for his son's disappearance, the young man's father quit politics in order to spend all of his time looking for his son. He used up most of a considerable fortune following any lead, no matter how dubious, driving and flying all over the country over the course of the next five years. The frustration of this fruitless mission began to take its toll, both financially and emotionally. The young man's parents were forced to sell their huge home and move into a small house in a run-down part of the city. They both began to drink heavily, which undoubtedly played a significant role in the automobile accident in which they were killed.

It was thought by many that the funeral of his parents would be the incentive that would bring the young man out of hiding and back to our city. However, it is not known whether or not he even learned of their deaths, because he never showed up. Many assumed that he, too, had died: a victim of the streets.

Each year our local newspaper now runs a story about this mysterious young man and how his disappearance may have inadvertently changed the course of our nation's history; a speculative piece full of why's and what if's about how different things might have been had his father stayed in politics and been elected President, an assumption that seemed to gain more certainty after his death than it ever had while he was alive. And this story would have slipped into the status of nothing more than interesting local legend had a caretaker at the cemetery not noticed the objects on the grave of the young man's parents. He found two fresh white roses and a small sign made from a piece of cardboard. The sign, printed with black marker, read: "Please Help. Anything Will Do. God Bless." A handwriting expert studied the sign and concluded that, based on a comparison to samples from old college notes, it was nearly certain that the sign had indeed been written by the couple's son. The freshness of the roses, too, indicated that the items had been placed that same day.

Nothing else has ever been found on the grave, and it's been two years since the flowers and sign were discovered, but many people here (including myself) find themselves stopping now whenever they see homeless persons. We give them money while studying their faces, each of us certain we'll be the one to discover, at last, the missing college student.

3

Twelve years ago my wife and I bought a house beyond the northern limits of the city. We loved this house as much as people can love such things, and shared enjoyment and pride in taking care of it over the years. It sits atop a rise on a large, wooded lot in what was, at the time we moved in, a planned development. While not restricted in the way a gated community would be, its exclusivity stemmed from simple economics: the average family couldn't afford these properties. And, technically, neither could we. But we were young, childless professionals who harbored unbridled optimism concerning our future and figured that if we struggled a little for a few years, our success would soon provide the means to transform our home from a financial burden to a sound investment. As it turned out, we were right. In less than five years, both my wife and I were earning six-figure salaries.

The most appealing of the house's attributes was the most basic—location. It was outside the city in a rustic section of the county, yet our development's entrance was situated on a main highway connecting with the Interstate, which provided quick access to anywhere in town. Most days I could leave our house and be in my downtown office in less than fifteen minutes. To this day, despite the insidious advance of the city limits, the house enjoys relative isolation accorded by a buffer of untouched woods that surround the small, private community. And although I witnessed increasing growth along the highway as I made my daily commute to work, the only intersecting road close to the house was a narrow, dirt lane that curves into the woods, remarkable to me only as a valuable landmark that I used when giving directions to our place, since it is exactly eight-tenths of a mile from the entrance to the development.

Like so many things that our eyes stop seeing after they become familiar, I soon stopped noticing this unmarked road as I sped past on my way to and from town. There were never, that I have witnessed, any cars going down or coming from it, and I unconsciously assumed it was an old hunting path or shortcut to some place I never even bothered trying to imagine.

One Saturday six months ago, our daughter (who is two weeks from turning seven as I write this) was riding in the back of our minivan. I'd just picked her up from a friend's birthday party and she was unusually quiet. I assumed she'd worn herself out playing and, in fact, she seemed droopy-eyed when I peeked at her in the rearview mirror. So it startled me when, passing the dirt road, she asked if we could stop and walk down it. I started to ask why, but instead made a U-turn at the entrance to our development, and parked on the narrow gravel shoulder across from the path.

The early December sky was a brittle blue with big puffy clouds barely moving. The air was crisp without being cold, the kind of air that brings everything into sharp focus. As we walked along the hard, red clay road, I held my daughter's hand. The road curved to the right and then again to the left, disappearing deep into the woods. We hadn't gone more than half a mile when I could no longer hear cars from the highway. I glanced down at my daughter, who looked up and smiled, but I couldn't tell if it was an excited or a nervous smile.

We ventured farther into the woods, the naked maples and oaks standing in harsh contrast to the durable green of the pines. The trees seemed to close around us, and the road's end was nowhere in sight. I mentioned to my daughter that it was likely the road was a dead end and that we'd probably seen most, if not all, there was to see. And had I stopped right there and turned us around, I know things would be different now. But we kept walking just a bit farther, rounding another bend, and that's when we saw the house.

Actually, my first impression was that it was no more than a shack, perhaps indeed a hunting blind, bolstering my initial suspicion about the purpose of the road. Except that a thin, steady line of smoke rose from a pipe vent that angled up from the tin roof. The walls of the structure were simple boards and I could not see any windows. I stared at the ramshackle building, trying to reconcile my assessment that no one could possibly live in such a place with the sight of the smoke streaming from the chimney. I was about to tell my daughter that we needed to turn back when a man carrying an armload of sticks and branches came around the far side of the house. He was thin and walked bent forward, like the burden of the sticks was great. From where we stood, his eyes were no more than shadows set deep in his face above the sharp ridges of cheekbones that were, to my reckoning, sickeningly prominent.

When he noticed us, the old man stopped briefly, then continued into the house with his load of kindling. I waited to see if he would come back out to find out who we were once he'd relieved himself of his load, but he didn't. I looked at my daughter and could see the unspoken questions in her eyes. We turned and walked back to the car. Once buckled in her seat, my daughter asked me if I thought the man actually lived in that house. I said I doubted it, telling my first real lie to her.

I was unable to shake the image of the gaunt stranger (my neighbor, I realized), and for weeks, whenever I passed the dirt road, I would slow down, hoping to catch a glimpse of him. My daughter seemed to forget about the man in the flimsy shack and we never again spoke of him. I didn't mention him to my wife.

In late January our area was hit with an ice storm. For two days I didn't sleep, worried about the man in the woods. Once, in the middle of the night, I even climbed into my SUV and drove to the road and started walking down it, but chickened out, compounding my guilt and anxiety.

I know I should just take a walk down the dirt road and see for myself that the old man is fine. But I keep asking myself, what if he isn't? Who knew he was there—and could have helped him—besides me? Is it worse to know, or not to know? These questions paralyze me. And now my lack of sleep has begun to take its toll; I've become irritable. My wife and I fight often about little things; about nothing. I haven't been able to concentrate at the office and today my boss suggested I use some vacation time to get myself together. I'm thinking of quitting instead.

I don't know what I'll do or where I'll go if that happens, but I do know that, no matter what, I won't complain.

SPRING PLANTING

When I hear the faint crunch of gravel at the bottom of the driveway, there is no more than a trace of pink where the sky meets the edge of the newly planted tobacco field across the road. The air is hot, hotter than usual for spring, and sounds carry farther, so I know it'll be nearly a minute before Ethan's faded and dented pickup will crest the hump of the drive just beyond the gate. Despite this, my hand reaches for the shotgun lying across my lap.

The smell of coming rain is strong through the screen door where I've parked my chair so I'll have a clear view of the gate. I am glad; it hasn't rained in almost three weeks and the new tobacco plants need it. Holding on to the day's last light like a stingy child, the sky is the color of ashes. The escalating sound of tires sliding over loose stones stops abruptly and, when I squint, I can just make out the shape of Ethan's truck on the other side of the fence. I lift the gun and balance the barrel with my left hand. Several minutes pass with no movement from the pickup. Behind the house, a chuck-will's-widow calls his name from the edge of the trees. In front of the tobacco barn, bats plunge in graceful arcs to get their fill of the season's first mosquitoes. I keep still, confident I'm invisible in the darkness of the house.

When I hear the squeak of the car door's rusted hinges, I sit up and slide my hand along the gun's stock until I feel the trigger guard. In spite of the heat, the metal is cool against my finger. Ethan is just a moving shadow, but I watch him climb the gate, the metal moaning under his weight. I make out the silhouette of his own shotgun swinging from his right hand as he approaches the house.

"Ben Hoffman, you in there? This here's Ethan Stiny. We need to talk."

"Ben's here, Ethan," I say. "But he ain't comin' out, so you'd best just head on back home now."

I watch his head shift back and forth, trying to locate me, giving me confidence that I'm still hidden, and offering me a slight advantage for the time being.

"Now, Rachel, this is between us men. You stay out of it."

"I don't know. If you think about it, it has a great deal to do with me, don't you think?"

"I suppose so, but the settlin' is going to be by Ben and me. I don't aim for you to get hurt." His outline inches toward the porch.

"Neither do I, Ethan, but the fact of the matter is, Ben's not coming outside. And I feel it's my obligation to remind you that, right now, you are trespassing on our property, so if *you* don't want to get hurt, just turn around and get back in your truck and head out of here."

"Can't do that, Rachel. You know what he done."

"Yeah, I do. I can't really say I see what the attraction is, but what's done is done, I guess."

Ethan stops walking. He is about five feet from the bottom porch step and looking right at me. He's gotten close enough to see me—and my gun—through the screen door. A series of loud pings on the tin roof tells me that the rain has arrived.

"You need to reconcile this with Elizabeth," I say. "Ben's already told me he doesn't plan on seeing your wife again. And, for what it's worth, I believe him."

"Well, you're dumber than I thought, Rachel. And you don't need worry that I 'reconciled' with Elizabeth. If you was to see her right now, you'd see the reconcilin' all over her." He wipes rain out of his eyes and puts his foot on the bottom step. "Now I'm getting wet out here, so I don't want any more bullshit. Send that chickenshit husband of yours out here right now so we can be done with this thing!"

The shotgun blast echoes in the quiet house, and the smoke blinds me. I stand and wave my arm to clear the air. Through the hole in the screen, I see Ethan lying on the ground, pressing his left hand against his shoulder, trying to stop the bleeding. I push open the screen door with my foot, its usual creaking lost in the ringing in my ears. I keep the gun aimed at Ethan as I walk down to where his own gun has fallen and kick it across the damp dirt of the yard.

"That was the last warning shot you get," I say. Ethan lies shaking and even though it is now full dark, I'm close enough to see his face has lost its color. "Do you think you can get up?"

He nods slowly and groans as he bends at the waist, managing to get into a sitting position. A bat swoops close to his head and then moves off across the tobacco field. Ethan slips twice trying to stand, so I grab his good elbow to help him to his feet. The rain has made his skin slick and he nearly falls. I step back and level the shotgun at his belly. I shake my head to clear the rain from my face.

"This ain't done, Rachel. Not by a long shot." His right arm is covered with blood and in the warm, wet air I can smell the iron-y thickness of it.

"It's over, Ethan. Be reasonable, you hear? I'd better not see you near this place again, or you'll be dead before you cross that gate. Now go home and tend to your cheating wife, and let me tend to my cheating husband."

"We'll see what the sheriff has to say about all this."

"Fine. But until then, get the hell off my property." I cock the hammer on the unused barrel.

Ethan sways and I know he wants to say more, but he is getting weak and leaking blood and realizes he'd better get some medical attention, quick. He starts walking toward where his shotgun has landed under an azalea bush on the side of the house.

"No, sir," I say. "You leave that gun right where it is."

He doesn't look at me or try to challenge me, just turns and lurches toward the gate. By the time he reaches it, he is lost in the blackness. I stand in the rain, listening to him fumble with the chain and eventually hear the low moan of the metal once again as he climbs over. The truck's door slams and it is several minutes before I hear the engine start up. When Ethan pulls on the headlights, they are aimed right where I am standing, lighting me up like I'm onstage. Blinded to him by the bright beams, I nod, knowing he can see me clearly. The truck backs away slowly, and the lights bounce as it goes over the bulge in the ground. Soon, I can no longer see or hear the pickup.

I lower the shotgun to my side and rub the ache in my right shoulder from holding it up so long. I head into the house, letting the screen door slam behind me. In the kitchen, I find a dish towel to dry my face and to soak as much rain from my hair as possible. Then I go toward the back of the house, to the mud room, where Ben is. I think about how Ethan said Ben is a chickenshit coward, and it pains me to realize how true that is. After eight years of marriage, it is heartbreaking to find out the man I love with all my heart is not who I think he is. Not even man enough to just admit he's been whoring around with that no-good, slutty Elizabeth Stiny, even after I tell him Maeve Cox has seen him, plain as day, humping Elizabeth in the backseat of her LTD behind the Piggly Wiggly.

In the mud room, I swat at flies and push open the back door, jamming a stick underneath to prop it open. I slide the tarp off Ben and stare down at his body. Even in the absence of regret, I wince at the gaping hole in his crotch. Stringy tissue hangs from the wound, making me look up, toward the hole in his chest, which somehow looks neat compared to the mess below it. Ben's face is oddly calm, so unlike how it looked just before I called him on his lies.

I smell the rain again and look out into the black night, grateful for the water soaking the tobacco field, bringing life to the delicate early plants and softening the ground there to make the work ahead easier.

SHRIMP ARE BORN DEAD

Looking back, the goodbye was in Miranda's eyes long before she actually got around to telling me she was leaving.

It was a Sunday in late August. I was stretched out on the sofa, busy with the *Times* crossword. Doing pretty well with it, too, until she dropped the bomb on me. Now I can't remember if I ever finished the puzzle.

"Rick, we need to talk."

"Hold on a sec. Do you know a twelve-letter word for Byzantine theater? Begins with S, I think." I tapped the eraser end of the pencil against my chin.

"This is important, Rick. Put down the puzzle." Miranda stood to the side and slightly behind the sofa, so that I had to twist my neck to look at her.

"What is it?"

"I'm leaving you," she said. "Right after the beach trip. I don't want to spoil that for the kids. But I've tried, Rick, I really have. I just can't stay here anymore." Her eyes, once the most beautiful shade of brown I'd ever seen, started to glisten, but no real tears came. "It hasn't felt right for a long time now."

I looked at the newspaper in my hand, at the half-finished

puzzle. "What hasn't felt right?" I asked, sensing I was supposed to say something, anything.

"Everything. Us, the kids, this life." She looked down and picked at a ragged fingernail. "You're a successful doctor and people respect you for that. Your patients love you. You get your research published in medical journals, and even other doctors look up to you. But what about me? What do I have? My claim to fame is being Mrs. Dr. Richard Sheridan. I know it sounds petty, but I'm thirty-five years old and I've accomplished nothing in my life. Nothing on my own, anyway. I deserve more than that."

"You're absolutely right, Miranda."

"You agree?"

"Yes. It *does* sound petty."

She stiffened and I could actually see her pupils constrict. I could tell this wasn't how she had scripted the scene, but I didn't really care. I expected tears at my comment, but none came.

"What about this house, Miranda? And the kids? You've built a good home. You ought to be proud of that."

"That's not enough. Not anymore."

I glanced down at the puzzle. A large block of empty spaces caught my eye and I had an urge to just fill them in with any letters, whether they formed words or not. When I looked back up, Miranda was biting her lower lip.

"Is there someone else?" I asked.

"Jesus, you really don't get it, do you?"

Miranda stood looking down at me for several moments. She hooked the sides of her short, brown hair behind both ears with a quick, jerky motion. Throughout the first ten years of our marriage her hair had been long, but she had it cut short about six months earlier. I wonder how many other clues I had missed. Or simply ignored. I felt like many of my patients, those who refuse to admit that the shortness of breath they've been experiencing is significant, or the sudden numbness in their arm might need to be looked at, acknowledging their chest pains only when they are lying on the kitchen floor and the EMT is ripping open their shirt, slapping the defibrillators down and jolting reality into them.

After Miranda had walked away I remained on the sofa a long time, numb and confused. The sunlight slanting in from the big, arched window traversed steadily across my body, silently mocking me by moving while I was unable to do so. The oddly ordinary sounds of our life—the kids upstairs, playing a computer game with its constant beeping and buzzing; Rosie, outside, barking at the neighbor's cat; Miranda's footsteps through the ceiling above me as she walked across the bedroom floor—entered my ears dull and muted, as though filtered through gauze, yet took on shattering importance in my mind.

The following day we left for the beach. Each year, since before Emily and Danny were born, we rent the same two-story beachfront house at Wrightsville Beach. Outwardly, the four-hour drive was a picture of normalcy. Miranda read a romance novel, at times laughing at something in the story, while the kids either dozed or played in the backseat. It was almost as though I, alone, realized things were different, and I caught myself wondering if I had only imagined Miranda's declaration of independence the day before. But these doubts were firmly erased as we settled into the beach house. Emily and Danny ran to put their bags in the small gabled room on the top floor they always used, but Miranda placed her things in a small extra bedroom, one with only a single bed, leaving me the master bedroom to myself.

That first night I lay, by habit, on my usual side of the queen-sized bed, listening to the rhythmic sound of the waves through the open window. Sleep eluded me. My thoughts undulated with the breakers, gathering with their swell and scattering with their crash against the sand. The flat, salty air sharpened my senses, and I felt the changes in my life that were just beginning were both vivid and indistinct at the same time. I thought of the

ancient explorers who had sailed across the very ocean I was
hearing, and I understood the fear and uncertainty they'd surely
faced.

For the first couple of days I moved like an actor in a play
of my own life. The four of us did all the things we had always
done on our vacations: the mornings spent at the beach, the
kids swimming and playing in the surf while Miranda and I lay
half-dozing in our beach chairs, pretending to read paperbacks;
the afternoons occupied by board games, naps or visits to local
sites. In the evening Miranda cooked dinner while the children
and I walked along the water's edge collecting shells and waiting
for the day's last light to fade from the horizon. Danny and
Emily, oblivious to their parents' rift, romped and squealed with
happy ignorance. That was exactly what Miranda had planned,
and I played along for their sake.

The third day, I was standing in the driveway, hosing sand
off the kids' rafts, when I heard Miranda and Emily coming
down the steps behind me. Their hair was still damp from
showers and they both wore yellow tee shirts, cutoffs and flip-
flops. At five, Emily, other than her longer hair, was nearly an
exact, if miniature, version of her mother. Emily ran up to
me and begged to use the hose. I handed it to her as Danny
bounced down the steps, his hair dripping stripes down his
gray tee shirt. As soon as he saw his younger sister with the
hose they began to squabble over who got to use it. I turned
to Miranda, who was watching the children. Her eyes were
moist, with real tears this time. She caught me looking at her
and the expression vanished, replaced by the bland emptiness
I was getting used to.

"We're going shopping to get stuff for dinner," Miranda said.
"I'm craving crab, so I called Benny's and they've reserved half
a dozen blue crabs for me. I'll get some shrimp for you. Is there
anything else you want while we're out?"

"Do we have enough beer? That's all I can think of."

"Aren't you coming with us, Daddy?" Emily, having given

up the fight for the hose, walked over and took my hand. The honest sweetness of both the gesture and the question was nearly too much for me.

"If you want me to I will," I said, not looking in Miranda's direction.

"Danny, Daddy's coming with us!" Emily shouted.

Danny, already bored with cleaning the rafts, dropped the hose and ran to where the three of us stood. Water from the hose flowed down the smooth white cement and splashed around our feet. I went over to the spigot and turned it off. We piled into the Volvo and drove to Benny's Seafood, a parody of the perfect American family.

Benny's was about halfway between Wrightsville Beach and Wilmington, down a narrow dirt trail off Eastwood Road, unmarked save for a small, hand-painted white sign with blue letters that said "Fresh Seafood." When I made the turn off Eastwood, the car kicked up a plume of dust behind us and I winced at the frequent pings of pebbles kicked up against the sides of the station wagon. The long, gravel road arced to the right until it dead-ended at the intra-coastal waterway. Sitting at an angle next to a weathered pier, like an afterthought, was Benny's wooden shack. The place looked abandoned when I pulled up and parked by the front door. As I walked up the board steps, I noticed several gulls looping overhead, waiting for the inevitable feast of fish heads and other waste that, no doubt, appeared with some regularity from Benny's back door.

Inside, the musty odor of fish and seafood overpowered me. With the exception of shrimp, I dislike fish and other seafood and find the smell unpleasant. I imagine, however, that to those who love seafood, like Miranda, the smell of Benny's is delightful.

"Ooh. It smells fishy in here," Emily said.

"That's because it's a *seafood* store, dummy," Danny said, and thumped his little sister on the head with a flick of his middle finger.

"OWW! That hurt!"

"Kids, please stop it," Miranda said. She began looking into several of the many large coolers placed around the walls of the small room.

"Hi, can I help you?"

I turned to see a young man with a goatee and sandy blond hair tied back in a ponytail emerge from a room to my left. He was wearing a shiny white plastic apron that was liberally splattered with red and brown stains.

"Yes, thank you," Miranda said. "The name is Sheridan. We called in an order for crabs and shrimp."

"Hold on and I'll check."

When the young man disappeared into the back, I walked over to where Emily was tapping on a large clear plastic tank. Inside the tank, about two dozen blue crabs scrambled over each other in an effort to be on top.

"Look how pretty they are, Daddy." Emily pressed her hand against the plastic and the nearest crabs tried to move away from it.

"Yes, they are, honey."

The young man reappeared carrying a styrofoam cooler and walked over to the tank which Emily and I were looking in. "Half dozen crabs. That right, sir?"

"Yes," Miranda said, coming up behind us. "The biggest you have."

I saw Emily's face register the realization that we were about to take some of the crabs she had been admiring. Her eyes, large and frightened, looked up at me. "Are we going to eat these crabs, Daddy?"

"Well, Mommy and you and Danny are. I don't like crab, honey."

"But . . . doesn't that mean we have to *kill* them?" Mercifully, she had turned toward Miranda.

Miranda looked at me, but I turned to watch the young man reaching expertly into the tank to grab our six crabs. "Yes, Emmy, it does," she said. "A lot of the things we like to eat have to be killed so we can eat them."

"Well, I don't want to eat crabs then," Emily said, folding her arms.

"That's fine, honey," Miranda said. "You don't have to eat any if you don't want to."

The young man placed the lid on the cooler and took it over to a small counter across the room. "Let's see. You wanted a pound of shrimp, too." He went over to one of the freestanding cooler chests and began scooping handfuls of shrimp into a thick plastic bag. Once again, Emily turned to her mother.

"What about the shrimp, Mommy? Do we have to kill them, too?" Emily's voice sounded fragile, like balsa wood.

Miranda, who I suspect had realized the question was coming, answered immediately. "No, dear. Shrimp are born dead."

The relief on Emily's sweet face was palpable. "I'm glad. That way they never have to hurt when we cook them."

Danny, three years older than his sister and well beyond the years of believing everything his parents told him, began to laugh. I shot him a look that shut him up and made clear that the subject was closed.

No one spoke as we drove back to the beach house. In the quiet car the only sound was the crabs scratching at the sides of the cooler. I glimpsed Emily's sad, thoughtful face in the rearview mirror. I noticed she kept turning to look behind her seat, at the cooler of crabs.

Just before crossing the bridge to the island, I made a sudden right onto Wrightsville Avenue and pulled off the road next to a low-lying marshy area adjacent to the intra-coastal waterway.

"Why are you stopping here?" Miranda asked.

"I think we need to let the crabs go," I said.

"Really, Daddy?"

"Yes, Emmy. Unless your mom objects, that is."

I held Miranda's eyes for a moment. She looked away first, turning toward Emily.

"I don't think any of us can cook these crabs, honey. Your daddy's right. We should set them free."

The four of us got out of the car. I opened the back of the station wagon and lifted the cooler of crabs, its weight shifting as the crabs scrambled around inside. I led my family in a line to the water's edge, like some strange reverse funeral. The crabs on top of the pile waved their claws frantically when I picked them up, and disappeared quickly from sight when put on the muddy slope next to the water. The two crabs that were on the bottom, which had been most deeply embedded in the crushed ice, were sluggish from the cold and, once in the water, listed like shipwrecks, floating more than swimming. Emily jumped up and down, cheering the crabs as they moved toward their newfound freedom. I watched her unbridled enthusiasm and could not help being touched by it. As I looked at her, at her uncanny resemblance to her mother, I saw not merely the possibility but rather the inevitability of her growing up to look exactly like Miranda. I looked down at the last crab, now beginning to move as the warm water reversed its cryogenic state, and smiled at the unexpected second life I had given it.

"Can we go now, please? I want to go swimming again before dinner," Danny said at last, ending our impromptu ceremony.

We climbed back into the car and I made a U-turn to head for the bridge to Wrightsville Beach. As I turned right at the end of the road, I noticed an old man in hip waders beneath the bridge, standing in the water up to his knees. I watched him toss a crab net onto the water. Emily, who was busy with a coloring book, hadn't noticed the man. I shook my head at having reinforced her development as a compassionate person, while, at the same time, offering a prize catch for the unknown crabber beneath the bridge.

Three days later we left for home, and two weeks after that Miranda had packed most of her things and moved into a small rental house on the other side of Winston-Salem. Within two months she enrolled in the pre-nursing program at the University of North Carolina at Greensboro, thirty minutes away, and announced her intention to become a registered nurse.

If I had been surprised by Miranda's sudden announcement that our marriage was over, I was equally surprised by my easy acceptance of it. I'm sure Miranda expected some effort on my part, some begging for her to stay, but our separation seemed natural to me, like a small stream that forks suddenly, each new half flowing effortlessly in its new direction without resistance or turbulence. I had come to realize that inertia, rather than love and affection, had been the glue that had held us together.

We worked out a quick, fairly amicable separation agreement. I agreed to almost all of Miranda's conditions and, since we lived so close to each other, custody arrangements were easy to split evenly. Danny and Emily adapted far more readily to life in two homes than I would have imagined. But that's not to say they were unaffected.

One chilly October Saturday three weeks after Miranda had moved out, it rained hard. I was in the kitchen, making grilled cheese sandwiches for lunch, when I heard a repeated banging and another sound, a grunt or groan, from the backyard. I looked out the kitchen window and saw Danny, barefoot and wearing nothing but his tee shirt and underpants, swinging a hammer against the bicycle Miranda and I had given him for his birthday in the spring. The front wheel of the bicycle was bent beyond repair, with several spokes sticking out at odd angles. I watched my son for several minutes until I saw the frequency and urgency of his swings diminish. I hurried upstairs to get a blanket and by the time I got outside, Danny had dropped the hammer and was bent over the smashed bicycle, sobbing. I wrapped the blanket around his small, bony shoulders and pulled him against me. He resisted at first, but then grabbed me and we stood holding each other tightly, letting the rain soak us. When his crying slowed I carried him into the house and up to his room, changed his underwear and put him in bed. We never spoke. I sat on the edge of his bed until he fell asleep, and then changed into dry clothes myself.

It's been nearly a year since Miranda left me, and while I have managed my life into a comfortable routine, I still find myself wondering about the hole in my life where she used to be. But not with a sense of regret for not having her with me, rather a peculiar marveling at the effortless way we blind ourselves to life's possibilities. I plan to take Danny and Emily to Wrightsville on our annual beach vacation soon. I know it won't be the same, but I anticipate it nonetheless. I'm looking forward to swimming in the rough surf, like a Hindu marching toward the Ganges. If I am not exactly reborn, then at least I will have reached another milestone and continued on.

But sometimes at night I lie alone in the dark, and in that moment just before sleep when wishes and fears and dreams all float loose and fuse together, I find myself imagining that I will just lie on Danny's raft and let the current take me steadily away from the shore, until there is nothing around me but the smell of brackish water and the heat rising off my sun-tortured skin. And while I drift alone on the ocean, I imagine below me thousands, maybe millions, of shrimp swimming free from care, delighted simply because they are not born dead.

A House Divided

My sister, Abigail, is in love with Abraham Lincoln. I don't mean a reverent fascination with his writings or accomplishments, but an honest-to-God, giggly schoolgirl crush. She thinks Abe's hot. Walking into her bedroom is like stepping into the souvenir shop at Ford's Theater. Photos of Abe plaster every wall, like he's some nineteenth-century rock star. Lincoln biographies and related knickknacks cover every surface in her room. Abby spent an entire Saturday going from junkyard to junkyard just to find an old Illinois license plate imprinted with "Land of Lincoln."

Don't get me wrong. I love Abby, but as an older sister who should be my role model, she leaves a little something to be desired. Heck, maybe a lot. And while I've accepted that she's harmlessly eccentric, if a bit annoying, and our mother has stopped wringing her hands and now just hopes that Abigail's crazy phase will soon pass, the biggest foe of my sister's unconventional romance has been our father.

Gerald Allan McCurdy is a man of routine. For as long as I can remember, my father has followed a single daily ritual. He rises at five o'clock in the morning to head downstairs to the coffeemaker, his heelless leather slippers flapping loudly as he walks past my bedroom. Once the coffee's going, it's back upstairs for a shower. After he's dressed, he pours his coffee into a double-sized mug and then he heads out for the ten-minute drive to his office.

My dad, like Abraham Lincoln, practices law. As best as I can tell, he sits in his office all day reading contracts, scratching out words here and there, scribbling notes in the margins, and flipping through law books. It all looks extremely boring to me, but Dad insists that what he does is quite important because if he does his job well, he can save people untold misery, not to mention thousands of dollars. I guess I'll just take his word on that.

At five-thirty each evening Dad comes home and swaps his suit for khaki pants and a polo shirt. He disappears into his den to sink into an overstuffed armchair where he reads mail and watches the evening news until Mom announces dinner.

In fact, it was at dinner one evening that Abby gave our family the first glimpse of the infatuation that soon consumed her. A new school year had just begun. Surprisingly, both Abby and I were excited about going back. I was beginning my first year of high school and it was the start of Abby's last. As it turned out, one of her first big school assignments was to research and write a biography of a randomly assigned figure from American history. I can only imagine how different the past six months would have been if Abby had been assigned Spiro Agnew or Clara Barton instead of Lincoln.

"Abigail! This is the last time I'm going to call you. If you don't get down here right now you'll get no dinner this evening."

That phrase, shouted by Dad, officially starts dinner each night. Gerald McCurdy insists that it is improper etiquette to begin eating before everyone is seated at the table. Yelling, however, is apparently just fine.

Abby has long blonde hair. She had always worn it in one of two styles: straight down or in a ponytail, so when she came downstairs to dinner that night with her hair put up in a tight bun, Mom, Dad, and I stared at her.

"What's everyone looking at?" Abby asked.

"Well, gee, let's see," I said. "Do you think it might be your bizarre Susan B. Anthony hairdo?"

"Nicole, that's enough," Mom said. "But in all honesty, Abby, we've never seen you wear your hair like that. Is there a reason?"

"Jesus! Why is everyone acting like a new hairstyle is a crisis?"

"Watch your tongue, young lady." Dad didn't tolerate even a hint of foul language from his daughters. "And no one is acting like it's a crisis. But you can't expect to do something completely out of character and not have people notice."

"I want to wear it this way, that's all." Abby scooted her chair up to the table. In her hand she held a folded piece of paper, which she slid onto her lap. "Can't we just eat?"

"What's that paper you're hiding?" Dad asked.

Abby's eyes shifted quickly from Dad to Mom to me to the paper. Her wide eyes reminded me of a trapped rabbit.

"Just part of my homework. Dinner sure smells good, Mother."

My parents and I exchanged puzzled glances. Never had I heard my sister refer to Mom as "Mother." I sensed something odd in the air besides the aroma of my mother's tofu "meatloaf."

"Then why are you hiding the paper?" Dad asked.

"I'm not hiding it."

"May we see it, then?" Dad held out his hand.

Abby looked down at her lap, contemplating. "It's just a picture."

Mom's head and my own turned in concert toward Dad, waiting for the next volley in their verbal ping-pong match.

"A picture of what, may I ask?"

Abby sighed. I sensed the turning of the tide in Dad's favor.

"It's just a photograph of President Lincoln I copied from a book," Abby said. "Are you happy?"

"My happiness is not the issue here, young lady. Your disrespectful tone, however, is. Now, I'd very much like to see the photograph so that we can get on with dinner."

"Why do you need to see it? You certainly know what he looks like."

"Abigail!" Mom said. "If your father asks you to show him that picture, then show it to him!"

Red splotches appeared on Abby's cheeks and neck, a sure sign of anger I've witnessed many times.

"'Broken by it I too may be; bow to it I never will,'" Abby muttered.

"What the heck is that supposed to mean?" I asked.

"Tyranny, dear sister. It's a quote from one of Abraham's speeches."

An awkward silence enveloped our dinner table. My mother and father exchanged looks that went beyond confused.

"Abby, let's try to put this minor insurrection behind us. Show me the paper on your lap and we can eat our dinner in peace."

Abby glanced again at the paper, looked at Dad and then back down. She pulled the paper up, sat fully upright and held it out to Dad. "'Of course, you expected to gain something by this request; but you should remember that precisely so much as you should gain by it others would lose by it.'" She turned toward Mom. "May I have some meatloaf, Mother?"

Our father, who took the crumpled paper, was, for the first time I'd ever seen, speechless. After a minute, he let his eyes fall on the sheet and, had I not been looking right at him, I would have missed the flash of shock in his eyes. In typical Gerald McCurdy fashion, he was able to gain composure quickly—he was not a man who allowed himself to be out of control—and slowly folded the paper in half before sliding it across the table to Mom.

Mom studied the picture but said nothing. Her face and neck, on the other hand, developed the same blotchy appearance as Abby's. In fact, it was uncanny how much Abby resembled our mother. Both have the same blonde hair, blue eyes, and fiery temperament. For my part, my parents' genetic stew had imparted to me my father's dark hair and complexion. Not to mention his lack of patience.

"Let me see!" I grabbed the paper from under Mom's hand. I unfolded it quickly, knowing I would be forced to return it right away. Abby shrieked, but I was determined to see what had shocked our parents. The paper contained a blurry reprinted photograph of a young Abraham Lincoln standing in front of a large white house. Across the face were lip prints in Abby's favorite shade of red lipstick. Drawn on the side of the picture was a heart containing initials, A.L. + A.McC.

Abby screamed, "Nikki! Give me that!"

"Nicole, give that paper to your sister this instant," Dad said.

Snickering, I handed the photograph to Abby, whose face had progressed from blotchiness to a uniform red.

"Wait until I tell everyone at school," I said, enjoying the special sense of power a younger sister gets when she possesses knowledge that can embarrass the hell out of an older sister.

"Well, Nicole, as Abe once said, 'I have endured a great deal of ridicule without much malice; and have received a great deal of kindness, not quite free from ridicule.' So do what you must, Sister."

Dad, about to sip his iced tea, froze with the glass tilted just short of his open mouth. His eyes shifted to Abby, then to me. I shrugged, holding my hands up. After a moment, the corners of his mouth raised and he nodded his head before taking a sip.

As it turned out, I didn't need to ignite gossip at school to embarrass my sister. Although Abby's antebellum style of dress and behavior soon became tolerated at home, there was no way she could maintain a façade of normalcy around a school full of teenagers. But to Abby's credit, she stuck with it. As Thanksgiving approached, so too did the deadline for presenting her biography project. And while our parents often voiced their hopes that Abby's history class presentation would mark the end of her "Lincoln thing," as they called it, it merely marked a new stage in my sister's strangeness.

The change started the day of her oral presentation. Abby went to school dressed in an ankle-length maroon dress, her hair done up in long, tight ringlets. She was quite stunning and, had the year been 1865, Abby would no doubt have caused a line of gentleman callers to form outside our house. Unfortunately, more than a century later, any would-be gentleman callers at West Forsyth High School laughed behind her back or made snide comments about her weirdness.

But that did not stop Abby from getting up an hour early each morning so she could fix her hair into long, tight curls and select just the right petticoat and dress for the day. She had scoured antique stores and vintage clothing shops until she had acquired what was certainly the largest private collection of nineteenth-century dresses and accessories anywhere in Lewisville, North Carolina. She was going to school everyday as though she was off to a new performance at Ford's Theater.

One evening the week before Thanksgiving, I was in my bedroom finishing my algebra homework when I heard the front door bang close. The digital clock on my desk confirmed it was five-thirty, the time our father arrived home. I listened for the creak of the wooden stairs from his customary heavy ascent up the uncarpeted steps. Reflexively, I counted the steps, knowing there would be eighteen. But at twelve the footsteps stopped abruptly. I was about to get up to check the hall when I heard the steps begin again, this time more quickly.

I heard a loud knocking on Abby's bedroom door. "Abby!"

I opened my door a crack, just enough to allow an unobstructed view down the hall. My father was holding a letter of some sort. He shook his head.

"Abigail, open up."

Her door opened slowly. Abby wore a long, high-necked flannel nightgown. Against her breast she clutched a book that I recognized as Carl Sandburg's biography of Lincoln. When she looked up at our father, her eyebrows arched primly.

"Yes, Father?"

"Abby. We need to talk. We just received a letter from school. Your teachers and counselors are beginning to worry about this obsession of yours. And to be quite honest, your mother and I are reaching our limit of tolerance for it as well."

"I'm not obsessed, Father. Anyone who doesn't conform to society's artificial standards of behavior is labeled a freak, or pigeonholed into some subcategory of mental illness."

"For God's sake, Abby, this is ridiculous. This is not about conforming to artificial standards. We are concerned that you don't lose touch with reality. You're an intelligent girl and surely know that how you've been dressing and acting is inappropriate."

"So, I suppose you'd prefer that I bare my midriff and get my navel pierced? Or maybe you think I should get a tattoo on my derriere, which is the normal way to dress these days."

"There's no need to be sarcastic, young lady. Your behavior has apparently become disruptive at school. You must be aware that your actions affect others. Nicole has suffered barbs from fellow students because of you. Many of my clients have children who attend your school. I won't have my own reputation tarnished because of your silly fascination, so I'm forbidding you to continue to dress as you have been. As long as you live in my house and eat my food you'll do as I say. Do I make myself clear?"

"Oh, yes. Perfectly, Father. I am as beholden to you as a slave to its master. But remember what Abraham said: 'It is my pleasure that my children are free and happy, and unrestrained by parental tyranny. Love is the chain whereby to bind a child to its parents.'"

Dad placed his hands on his hips. "Yes, well, Abraham Lincoln didn't have *you* as his daughter!"

Dad turned away and Abby slammed her bedroom door. Dad stopped, raised his hand to knock on the door, but changed his mind. As he walked down the hall to his own bedroom, I ducked back so he wouldn't see me eavesdropping.

"Did you enjoy the show, Nikki?" my father asked as he walked past.

"No, Dad," I said. "Sorry."

However, neither that proclamation nor the conclusion of Abby's school project marked the end of Abby's fixation with Lincoln. As Thanksgiving and Christmas came and went, our household settled into an uneasy peace punctuated only by sporadic skirmishes between Abby and Dad. Mom and I, for the most part, managed to avoid these battles, but I did get a lecture from Dad when I gave Abby her Christmas gift—a limited edition replica of an envelope with the words of the Gettysburg Address in Lincoln's handwriting, employing state-of-the-art computer-aided aging to give it the look and feel of actually having been written in 1863.

Like so many things that seem peculiar when you first observe them, Abby's aberrant behavior eventually became mundane at school. As the new year began, kids at school became bored by her oddness and she suffered fewer and fewer taunts. But, as we soon learned, the lack of overt insults did not mean no one gossiped about Abby behind her back.

Ironically, it was February 12, Lincoln's birthday, when a shift occurred in the course of life at the McCurdy household. The weather, which had been unseasonably mild for weeks, took a sudden turn as a cold front moved in and snow began to fall heavily. Again, it was during dinner that events changed. I was surprised that my father hadn't commented on the birthday cake sitting in the middle of the table. Abby had baked it that afternoon. It was square, with white icing and the words, "Happy Birthday, Abe" written with blue icing on the left side in Abby's handwriting. A small lopsided stovepipe hat was drawn next to the words. In fact, I noticed that my father was unusually silent. An undefined disquiet filled the room. He took furtive glances at the cake but said nothing.

"I wonder if school will be cancelled tomorrow." Mom pushed a piece of squash back and forth across her plate with her fork.

"I hope so. I have a math test," I said.

Dad, who under normal circumstances would have berated

me quickly for such a remark, continued to eat his dinner slowly.

"Would you girls like more casserole?" Mom scooped a large portion from the serving dish and held it up.

"No, thanks," I answered. I still had a plateful of zucchini and green beans.

"I've had sufficient supper, Mother. Thank you. May we cut the cake now?" Abby asked.

I looked quickly at Dad to see his reaction, but he just stared down at his plate. He scooped up the last bit of casserole with his fork, ate it, and wiped his mouth with his napkin.

"If you all will excuse me, I have some work to do in my study." Dad stood and walked out of the room.

After a brief silence, Abby began cutting the cake. Humming "Happy Birthday," she carved off one corner and passed it to me. She cut off the other and offered it to Mom, who folded her arms and glared at Abby with tight lips. Abby put the plate down and stopped humming. For her own piece, she carefully carved out the section saying "Abe." Abby and I ate our dessert in silence. Afterwards, she and I rinsed the dishes and loaded the dishwasher while Mom brought the last of the dishes in from the dining room.

"Will you girls finish the dishes, please?" Mom said. "I need to talk to your father." She handed me the leftover birthday cake and left the room.

"What do you think's going on with Mom and Dad?" Abby asked.

"Gee, I have no idea, Braniac. Do you think it might have to do with your little birthday party?"

"I mean, Dad's acting even stranger than usual, don't you think?" All traces of Abby's nineteenth-century persona were gone.

Abby was right, but I wasn't going to say that. "Stay here."

"Nikki, wait . . ."

I ignored her and crept down the hall leading to my father's den. The door was open and, as I approached, I could hear my parents' voices. I stopped at what I judged to be a safe distance for retreat should one or both of them suddenly emerge from the room.

"I just worry that there will be more," my father said.

"What do you think we should do, Gerald?"

"I don't know. Ed Brenner's firm is my second-largest account. Losing it would be a huge financial loss for us. And if what he says about Allan Myers also leaving is true, then that would be a significant blow to my firm."

"I find it hard to believe they'd be so childish and judgmental," Mom said.

"Reputation is everything in my business, honey. It may not seem right, but people like Ed and Allan don't want their own reputations sullied by association with anything or anyone they consider lacking in propriety. Abigail's behavior reflects on us. On me."

"Oh, like those little snobs Emily Brenner and Wendy Myers don't do enough on their own to embarrass their fathers. I'd like to get my hands on those petty, jealous little . . ."

"Calm down, Donna," Dad said. "You can't expect kids not to talk to their parents about something like this."

"I know. It just makes me so mad," Mom said. "Well, what do you plan to do?"

"I'm not sure. But I guess it's time to come to terms with this."

There was a long pause and I wondered what my parents were doing. I thought about trying to sneak a peek in the den but decided to hurry back to the kitchen. I kept expecting one or both of our parents to come into the kitchen, but they never did.

"What did you hear?"

I peeked out the kitchen door, but our parents were nowhere in sight. "Seems Wendy Myers and Emily Brenner have been talking to their parents about your Lincoln obsession—"

"I am *not* obsessed."

"Yeah, whatever. Anyway, it seems their dads are big clients of Dad's, and, well, because of you there's a chance they're going to stop doing business with his firm."

I noticed something shift in Abby's eyes. For the rest of the evening I sat in my room watching the snow fall outside my window, as I waited for Dad to approach Abby's room and lay down the law, once and for all. At last, I heard the slow, methodical sounds of my father's footsteps on the stairs. I braced myself and angled my chair so I could see. First, the top of his head, then, bit by bit, the rest of him appeared. He paused at the top of the landing, sighed, and approached Abby's door, his head down. She must have been waiting, because before he could knock, the door opened.

"Hi, Dad," Abby said. No "Father" this time, I noticed.

"Abby, I just wanted to say goodnight. And I wanted to tell you something important."

"What is it, Dad?"

"I know I don't say it very often, but I wanted to make sure you know that I love you very much." Through the slit of my door I saw Dad put his arms around Abby and hug her long and tight. "Goodnight, sweetheart."

As he turned and walked toward his own bedroom, I whirled my chair around pretending to be studying.

"I love you, too, Nicole," he said, as he passed my door.

"Um, I love you, Dad."

The next morning we found that there hadn't been enough snow to cancel school. Abby came downstairs to breakfast dressed again like a teenage Mary Todd. She smoothed the front of her skirt, a prim mannerism I still found annoying, though she'd been doing it for months.

"Your food is probably ice cold," Mom said. "I called you down almost twenty minutes ago."

"I'm sorry, Mother. I had trouble with my hair."

"For God's sake, Abby, stop talking like that! Enough is enough. When are you going to grow up and think of someone besides yourself?"

Abby's mouth dropped open. Since the beginning of her Lincoln phase, both Mom and I had tried to remain neutral in the skirmishes that flared between my father and sister.

Mom scraped the remains of scrambled eggs into the sink and banged the pan loudly onto the counter. She put the milk and margarine back into the refrigerator, and slammed the door closed.

"You'd better hurry up or you'll miss your bus," Mom said, then left the kitchen.

"Listen, Abby . . ." I said.

"Shut up! No one asked your opinion." Abby stormed out of the room.

That night, Dad was unusually quiet at dinner. I kept expecting him to take Abby aside and explain how her actions were affecting his business. I actually found myself wishing for one of Dad's outbursts, finding the silence far more frightening. I picked at my food.

Mom had fixed a penne pasta dish that was Abby's favorite and the aroma of tomatoes and mozzarella cheese filled the dining room as she carried the steaming entree from the kitchen. She placed it on the trivet in the center of the table, then glanced around to make sure she hadn't forgotten anything before sitting down.

"Dinner looks and smells delicious, Mother," Abby said, extending her plate so that Mom could spoon some pasta onto it.

"Thank you. Nicole, may I have your plate, please?"

When she finished with my plate, she filled Dad's and then her own. We ate quietly for five minutes. Then it came.

"Abby," Mom said. "Do you attend any classes with Emily Brenner and Wendy Myers?"

I stopped in mid-chew and looked at my sister. Her voice was shaky and barely audible. "Well, they're in my history class."

"I see," Mom said.

I glanced at Dad, who only nodded slightly, and lifted a stringy forkful of pasta to his mouth.

Abby opened her mouth, but closed it. She stared at her food for several minutes but didn't eat any more.

"If anyone needs me, I will be in my room for the rest of the evening," Abby said. She was looking only at Dad, though.

Later, I sat in my room listening to music, peeking out the door, anticipating Dad coming up the stairs to knock on Abby's door and, once and for all, issue the final decree that would end her weird infatuation with Abraham Lincoln. When at last I heard the sound of his footsteps, I jumped up and clicked off my iPod. To my surprise, however, when he reached the top of the stairs, Dad turned and walked past Abby's room toward his own.

"Good night, Nicole," he said, poking his head in as he passed my room.

"Good night, Dad."

The next day at school, I was scraping my lunch tray into the cafeteria trash can, dreading Ms. Hunsucker's English class, when I heard a commotion in the hall. Ashley Wellington, a snobby sophomore, burst into the cafeteria, laughing.

"Hey, everybody, come check it out!"

In the hallway, a large group of students was gathered near one of the main entrances. I joined them, but even on tiptoe I was too short to see what the fuss was about.

"What's going on?" I asked a tall boy with bad acne who was standing next to me.

"There's some old dude dressed like a Confederate soldier."

"You're kidding?"

I squeezed my way through the group, and got knocked around. I was not prepared for what I saw when I reached the front. Standing before me, asking dreamy Chad Matthewson for directions to Mr. Carlson's classroom, was my own father, a cheesy fake beard glued crookedly on his face. He tipped a plumed hat to Chad, adjusted the sash that actually held a sword, and proceeded along the North wing.

As I stood there, I wasn't sure whether I should hurry after Dad, or, as my instincts were telling me to turn and leave the building. Students pressed past me, following my father. I caught up with Dad when he was two doors away from Mr. Carlson's room. Embarassed, I ran up and grabbed his arm.

"Dad, what are you doing?"

He looked at me, smiled, then continued marching down the hall. "Pardon me, Miss, but ah'm on mah way to an important engagement, and mustn't tarry."

"Does Abby know about this?"

He didn't answer. Dad stopped to peek inside Mr. Carlson's room a second, before opening the door and striding in. I slipped in after him, closing the door on the curious crowd behind us. I tiptoed along the wall to stand at the back. Abby saw me, her eyes huge, and mouthed, "What the hell?" I held my hands up and shook my head.

Up front, our father stood at attention in his ridiculous get-up. He turned to Mr. Carlson.

"Ah beg your pardon at my intrusion, suh. Ah do not intend to take up much time, but Ah request a few moments to speak to your students."

Mr. Carlson rubbed his hand across his shiny, bald head, and bent forward to look over the top of his glasses. His eyes widened and then he smiled.

"Mr. McCurdy? What's this all about?"

Everyone in the room turned to look at Abby. Several students giggled. Abby, her face blotchy, sank in her seat. Wendy Myers actually rolled her eyes. She whispered something to Emily Brenner and they both pointed at Abby, shaking their heads. I felt my face flush.

"General Robert E. Lee, suh." Dad extended his hand toward Mr. Carlson, who hesitated before shaking it.

"Well . . . um . . . it's, uh, an honor to meet you, General."

"The pleasure is mine, suh. If it wouldn't be too much of an inconvenience, Ah request permission to briefly address your pupils."

Mr. Carlson nodded and gestured toward the class. Dad turned and bowed his head.

"Much, it seems, has been made about a certain student's eccentricities and the seriousness of their meaning. Some have even, Ah have found, been prone to spread petty gossip to their families, who in turn have, without renderin' benefit of doubt, cast aspersions on the entire family of said student. Ah, myself, have in fact been long engaged in a senseless and damaging civil war with this person. Indeed, Ah come before you today to publicly declare to her, Miss Abigail McCurdy, my unconditional surrender." Abby covered her face with her hands. "In a world where our children are easily caught up in painful and dangerous choices, I should never have made so much of such an innocuous oddness."

Then Dad walked over to Abby's desk, leaned down and kissed the top of her head. "I love you, Abigail. I am truly sorry. I nearly made a terrible mistake this week, but I have come to learn a simple truth, 'Never do a wrong thing to make a friend— or keep one.'"

Dad glanced over at Wendy Myers and Emily Brenner. Then he walked back up to the front of the room, bowed his head to Mr. Carlson.

"Ah thank you once again, suh, for your kind indulgence of mah intrusion. With a grateful remembrance of your kind and generous consideration of myself, Ah bid you all an affectionate farewell."

Then Dad marched to the door. Before he left, he looked at me and winked. Nobody moved or said anything for what seemed like forever. Finally everyone started talking and laughing, and Mr. Carlson kept shouting for quiet. When I snuck back to the door, I looked over at Abby, but she didn't see me. She had her face buried in her hands, and I could tell she was crying.

"Abigail and Nicole. If you don't get down here right now you'll get no dinner this evening."

Mom and Dad were already seated when I walked in. On the table was a covered serving dish and a large bowl of steaming rice.

As I took my place, I looked at Dad, who was smoothing his napkin on his lap and acting like his performance that afternoon at school had never occurred. Abby walked in the room, fidgeting with the fitted cuffs of her calico dress.

"You look lovely tonight, Abby," Dad said.

I stared at the alien who was sitting in my father's place.

"Close your mouth, Nikki," Mom said. She lifted the cover from a serving dish, revealing meatballs swimming in a dark, red-brown sauce. "Pass your plate, if you'd like some dinner."

"I got an interesting new client today," Dad said. He then proceeded to tell us in great detail about a not-actually-interesting case involving stocks and tax shelters and other boring stuff.

Even though General Lee was the talk of West Forsyth High for weeks, he was never mentioned in our home.

It's been two months since Lee's second surrender and things have now returned to their normal weirdness around our house. I'm sure that when Abby graduates and heads off to college this whole love affair with Abraham Lincoln will fade into a funny memory, but this morning she's asked me to go with her to one of her favorite vintage clothing stores to look for a new dress. A black one.

You see, tomorrow is April 15th. The anniversary of Lincoln's death.

THE FISH

I asked my father about the fish. It was the only thing Mom didn't take with her when she left us. We hadn't talked about her all day, Dad and I. Not a word since I explained to him last night how I'd found her cramming the last of the bulging Hefty bags into the back seat of the minivan when I got home from school yesterday; her driving off without a word.

She'd bought the fish nearly two years ago and kept it on the kitchen counter where she would sprinkle little flakes of food into its bowl every day and talk to it in a sing-song voice, as though it were a small child. Dad said, "Fuck the fish." He warned me not to feed it, said to just let it die.

After a couple weeks the water in the bowl had clouded to a brown-gray. I could barely see the bright blue fish gliding sluggishly through the murky liquid, spending most of the time at the top of the water. I imagined he, too, must be wondering where Mom had gone. I asked Dad several times why he didn't just get rid of the fish, flush it or something, but he would shrug or grunt and walk away. It occurred to me that he might be holding out hope that she would be coming back for it.

Dad took a long sabbatical from work. One evening, during a break from filling out college applications, I found him in the den staring at the television. The TV was tuned to ESPN, but the sound was muted.

"Dad," I said, standing next to the recliner, "she's only going to be more pissed off if she comes back and finds we tortured her fish."

He didn't take his eyes off the screen; a soccer game was being played somewhere in Europe. "Actions have consequences," he said. "Even your mother knows that."

Two weeks later was my Spring Break. I drove down to Myrtle Beach with my two best friends, but I called Dad every day. Our conversations, if you can call them that, lasted no more than a minute and consisted of me asking him how he was and him telling me he was fine. On the night before my return, when I made my usual call, he answered with "I found the fish food in your room," then hung up.

Dad was in the kitchen when I got home. He held out his right arm, the hand clenched into a fist. He unfurled his fingers to reveal the dried body of the dead fish, its long, flowing fins shriveled and curled like tiny blue commas.

"That's that," he said, before turning and dropping the shrunken carcass into the sink. He flipped the switch to start the garbage disposal and its roar replaced the awkward silence. Dad stood angled to me and I could see him staring down into the sink, his mouth moving, but I was glad I couldn't hear what he said. I walked out of the kitchen, out to my car to get my duffle before trudging upstairs to my bedroom. Even after I closed the door, I could still hear the rumble of the running disposal. It was a long time before it stopped.

EXTRACTIONS

He lies awake, unable to sleep, and listens to sleet battering the bedroom window. The room is dark and cold, the darkness cut only by the green glow of the digital clock on the table next to him. Beside him, Liz's soft, rhythmic breathing counters the sharp patter of the ice against the glass. He looks toward her, but she is invisible in the dim light. He leans close and catches the scent of her, a mix of her own natural smells and a flowery trace of soap. It helps dispel the uneasiness taking hold of him and he lies back down and closes his eyes.

He slips into a light sleep and for the fourth time that month has the same nightmare. In the dream, he is leaning over a boy, a dark-haired kid with a crewcut, whose wide, dilated eyes expose his fear. He tries to smile. *Everything's fine*, he says. He steps on the drill and touches it to one of the boy's teeth, but as soon as he does he senses something is wrong. The tooth shatters, tiny pieces of enamel shoot against his face, stinging him. The boy does not move. He touches the drill against another tooth, then another, again and again, until all the teeth have exploded, leaving the boy's mouth full of empty, red pockets. He stares at the mess and hears himself ask, *Where's the blood?*

The room is still dark when he awakens. He twists his upper

body to the right to check the clock. 5:08. The sleet is still hitting the window, but seems to have lost some of its intensity. He sighs and rolls onto his back. Above him, shadows move across the ceiling. He can't tell if they are real or imagined, the remnants of his bad dream.

He knows there is no point in trying to sleep anymore. He slides out of bed and dresses quietly. It is a few minutes before six when he opens the front door and steps onto the icy porch. The neighborhood is quiet beneath the dark, frozen clouds. Snow has begun to mix with the sleet. It's a short drive to the office, but he decides to walk, despite the weather.

He turns left onto Westview, three blocks from Stratford Road, taking care as he walks on the slippery sidewalk. All the houses he passes are large and expensive and dark. The leafless branches of the trees lining the way droop under the weight of a thick coating of ice. The streetlight reflects off the icy branches, lighting them like living chandeliers. He is glad he decided to walk.

When he reaches Stratford Road, he turns right and is a little sad to leave the peacefulness of the residential streets. Bright business signs seem especially glaring in the gloomy, wet morning—the green of Heyman's Jewelers, the blue of Blockbuster Video, the golden arches—incongruous in the muted monochrome of the winter storm. Behind him, he hears the rattle of tire chains, and turns to see a city truck pass as it drops a slurry of sand and salt.

A block later he reaches his office and fishes the key from his pocket. He glances at the sign above the door as he unlocks it. A blue square with white letters. "Family Dentistry. Eric S. Crowder, D.D.S. and Gina Blalock, D.D.S." Simple, the way he likes. Until five years ago, he had a nearly identical sign with just his own name that was the original sign he'd put up when he opened practice thirty-five years before. Stepping into the warm office, he marvels at how long, and yet how short, the time has seemed. Up until the past month he'd been excited about retirement, but now that his final day has arrived, he isn't so certain he's not going to miss it, after all.

He walks through the door separating the waiting area from the rest of the building and goes into the reception area to power up the computer. As was his routine for years, he next heads to the office's small kitchen to start the coffeemaker before going to his private office at the very back of the building.

When he switches on the light, the sight of the empty office hits him with an unexpected and profound sadness. He'd spent the past week packing his personal effects and books and moving them to the house, but he is still unprepared. In front of him sits his desk, cluttered for dozens of years, now bare except for a telephone. It seems at once unreal and frightening in its starkness. Two large bookcases, their shelves devoid of books, sit like skeletons against the walls on each side of the office's sole window behind the desk. He scans the walls in a slow arc, but these, too, are bare.

He walks behind the desk and opens the slats of the window blind. The sleet has picked up again and bounces off the frozen ground. Light from a tall lamppost reflects off a smooth sheet of ice that glazes the empty parking lot behind the building, its amber light filtering through the blinds to make wide stripes across the ceiling. He stares at the heavy sleet for a moment and wonders if they'll even open the office that day.

On the floor next to the desk's chair is a cardboard box he's filled with the last of the office's contents. He sits down and picks up a photograph poking from the box. He smiles at the young bride and groom, squinting against the sun. Surrounding the couple are the groomsmen, their tuxedos with wide lapels and even wider ties, and bridesmaids, all with matching Farrah Fawcett hairdos. He turns the photo over and reads the inscription. "Dr. Crowder, Thanks for making my wedding pictures perfect. You saved the day! Love, Lisa." He smiles, remembering the frantic phone call, and then meeting the distraught bride-to-be two nights before her wedding to repair a broken incisor. Somehow three-quarters of the tooth had broken off during an unexplained accident at her bachelorette party. He replaces the photo in the box amid an assortment of gifts, children's drawings and Play-Doh sculptures.

The smell of coffee drifts in from the hallway. Before carrying the box out, he decides to recheck the drawers of the desk. The large side drawers are empty. He pulls open the narrow middle drawer above the leg well. A scattering of paper clips and rubber bands litter several sheets of letterhead. He pulls the papers out and drops them onto the desktop. An envelope, yellowed and wrinkled, slides from among the sheets. Eleanor Roosevelt smiles from the faded 5-cent stamp in the upper right-hand corner. The envelope is addressed in an elegant script with a fountain pen. The ink was originally bright blue, he remembers, but is now a faint purple.

He turns the envelope over and reads the return address on the flap: 976 Sylvan Road, Winston-Salem, No. Carolina. There is no name above the address, but he knows, just as he had the day the letter arrived, who had sent it. A gust of wind rattles the window behind him and he jumps. The ice striking the glass picks up in intensity, as if it is frantic to get in. He flips the worn flap and pulls out the letter. The letter is long, four pages, and he hasn't read it in two years, but it is as familiar to him as the day he received it. He hears the distant sound of the city's truck passing back in the opposite direction on Stratford Road out front. He begins to read.

> *"Dear Dr. Crowder,*
> *My husband and I wish to thank you for your sweet letter.*
> *We are grateful, too, for the kindness and compassion you have*
> *shown us since our sweet Jimmy was taken from us."*

He lets the pages fall to the desk and leans back. For several minutes, his eyes fix on the orange bars of light crossing the ceiling, then close. In an instant, he is standing in his old exam room, where the kitchen is now, and he is looking at Jimmy Toscano, eight-years-old and terrified at his first visit to the dentist. He smiles at Jimmy and tells him everything's fine, even rubs the boy's crewcut head to calm him. *"You've got a badly infected tooth that needs to be pulled, Jimmy,"* he says. *"But I promise you won't feel anything. We're going to let you sleep through the whole thing. How will that be?"* The boy looks at him with eyes that remind him of a trapped rabbit. *"Will it hurt?"* the boy asks. He smiles and assures him it won't.

The scene freezes, like it is painted on the office's ceiling, and he looks away. His eyes drift around the empty walls, the ghost outlines of picture frames barely visible. He reaches to refold the letter, to slide it back into the envelope, but when he picks it up he finds the place he left off.

> *"I have heard from a friend that you have chosen, in light of Jimmy's death, to give up your practice. Please, Dr. Crowder, reconsider this decision. What a tragedy it would be, indeed, if this unfortunate accident led to the end of two lives."*

He has read the letter many times, but still his hand shakes as he holds it. Images flood his mind, unbidden, the same images that always come to him as he reads its words, as though they are the script to a movie he has seen over and over to the point of knowing each line, each action. Jimmy Toscano's small, frightened face relaxing as he administers the anesthetic. He turns away to arrange his instruments on a tray. He selects a root elevator, turns back to the boy and is frozen by the sight of Jimmy's pale blue skin and purple lips. His voice echoes as he yells for Colleen, his only assistant, who doubles as his receptionist. They work frantically to perform CPR while they wait for the ambulance. When the paramedics arrive they have to drag him off Jimmy so they can work. He stumbles back and sees Jimmy's mother standing in the doorway, her hands over her mouth, her eyes mirroring his own shock.

The memories speed up. He sees the months that followed Jimmy's funeral—his inability to work, his accelerated drinking, the investigation by the North Carolina Board of Dental Examiners and their final ruling that he was not at fault, that Jimmy simply had an unanticipated adverse reaction to the anesthesia. And his decision to quit. Last, he remembers Liz bringing in the mail one day, handing him the letter from Valerie Toscano.

He turns the pages over and traces his finger along the elegant script. His eyes follow its path until it stops on the final paragraph. He doesn't read the words, doesn't need to. The words, spoken in the soft, pained voice of Jimmy's mother, come to him anyway.

> *"Neither of us can change what God has chosen for Jimmy. Although his life has ended, yours is, in a great sense, just beginning. Live that life fully and well, Dr. Crowder. It is ironic to me that in life we are rarely able, no matter how hard we work toward them, to guarantee our successes, yet can quite easily choose our failures. Please use my sweet Jimmy's death to inspire you to always provide the best care possible for your patients. May God bless and keep you always."*

He stands and turns to the window. He holds the letter at his side. The sleet comes down in silver streaks, and as he watches it he knows he's already worked his last day.

With his free hand he reaches between the blind slats and touches the icy glass with his fingertips. *Karen Sizemore*, he whispers. She moved to Winston-Salem from Texas with her husband who had taken a job with Reynolds Tobacco. Mrs. Sizemore was in for a routine exam and cleaning and was unaware that she was his first patient after Jimmy Toscano's death. Everything went well with the exam, and the entire day. He took his work day-by-day for many months, and was able to slip into a routine that allowed him to run his practice.

He twists the rod and closes the blind. He folds the letter, replaces it in the envelope, and then slips it into his pants pocket. He phones his office manager and tells her to call the rest of the staff to inform them that the office will be closed due to the weather. The office manager is disappointed because they'd planned a small retirement party, but he promises that he'll come back soon so they can celebrate.

He stands in the doorway to his office and hesitates before turning off the light. He goes into the kitchen and switches off the coffeemaker. A large mug, shaped liked a molar, sits next to it. The mug is a gift from a client, but he can't remember which one. He picks it up and puts it in the box cradled under his arm. Once up front, he powers off the computer. Only then does he remember that he's walked to the office. He pushes the box of mementos under the desk in the reception area and scribbles a note that he'll come by to pick it up the following week. In the quiet office he can hear the crackle of the monitor as it shuts down. As he sticks the Post-it to the desk, the computer finishes shutting down but the crackling noise continues. It takes him a moment to realize he's hearing the light tap of the sleet against the front door.

When he walks outside, there is little time to contemplate the finality of leaving. The wind blows hard and he struggles not just to get his umbrella opened, but to keep it open. He points it in front of him like a shield against the sharp bite of the ice stinging his face. During his brief time inside, the sky has lightened and some people, by choice or necessity, have ventured outside. He moves forward against the wind, lifting the umbrella to check his path and get his bearings. It takes five minutes to walk the one block to Westview. When he makes the turn, his thighs ache, but he's relieved to be out of the headwind. His house is three blocks away, too far to see, but he stops and looks down the street. Despite heavy clouds, the early morning sky has muted the streetlights enough to diminish their magical effect on the ice-covered trees.

With the umbrella angled to his right, he plods along the

wet, messy sidewalk. The portions of his pants below his coat are soaked, clinging to his legs. He is shivering and miserable and unsettled. An SUV passes from behind, surprising him, and sprays slush around his feet. He hesitates, but when he looks up he sees his house only a block away.

He crosses the street with renewed energy, hoping Liz is still asleep so he can crawl back into their warm bed and snuggle her awake. His boots are soggy and in his haste he nearly slips walking up the brick path leading from the sidewalk to their front door. He rests the umbrella's handle on his shoulder and wiggles his fingers into his wet pocket for his keys. He feels the damp envelope and pulls it out. Several large drops of water splash onto it from the eave overhead. The ink runs in purple streaks along the paper. In seconds, the entire envelope is soaked. He drops the umbrella next to his feet and attempts to remove the letter. The pages are heavy and wet and the writing is blurred. He hunches over them, to shield them, but rain falls from his hair, large drops which explode against the paper, sending purple streams down the sheets. He peels them apart, but they tear in the process. His fingers are covered in ink. His eyes find isolated words—*compassion, darling, failures*—but these disintegrate with the rest.

He holds the sodden mass, no longer readable or salvageable, in his palm. It feels heavy. Shivering as sleet hits the back of his neck, he wads the remains of the letter in his hand.

In the entryway, he removes his coat and boots and drops them on the floor. The house is dark and quiet; Liz is still asleep. He goes into the kitchen and lets the warmth of the house soak into him. At the pantry, he stands for a moment looking at the sodden mass in his open palm, and then drops it into the trash can.

He walks across the room and, for the second time that morning, he measures coffee and fills the coffeemaker with water. He presses the start button and hears footsteps through the ceiling. He takes two cups from the cabinet and waits for the coffee to brew. He fills the cups, adds sugar and cream to Liz's, and heads upstairs to change into dry clothes.

FAMILY TREE

I killed my father. I've never said that to anyone; not in those words, anyway. I was ten and he was forty-one, the age I am now. Technically, my father's death was an accident, but all along I've known my part in it. It happened on a cold, sunny Monday in February in front of the house in northern Connecticut where I grew up. It had snowed hard all weekend and school had been cancelled. My older brother, Mickey, and I were making the best of the unexpected vacation. We hauled the matching Flexible Flyer sleds we'd gotten for Christmas from the basement and were flinging ourselves down the long, steep street atop which our house sat. As we trudged up the slippery road to make another run, I noticed my father watching us through the big picture window of the living room, absently swirling his first scotch and water of the morning with a crooked grin on his tired face. It was no small surprise to Mickey and me when he emerged through the front door, struggling to catch the zipper of his parka. "Let me have a turn, Tommy," he said, gesturing toward the sled dragging behind me. I looked at Mickey, who was sitting on his own sled, already scooting toward the edge of the drop-off. He shrugged and then was gone down the hill.

As I looked at my father swaying unsteadily, his gloveless hands buried in his armpits and his breath puffing out in quick, scotch-reeking mists, my instinct was to swing the Flexible Flyer around, hop on it, and fly away down Shaker Road, leaving Mickey to deal with our father's request when he got back up top. Instead, I handed my father the rope to my sled. He walked to the middle of the road, picked the sled up by the sides, jogged to the start of the slope, shouted over his shoulder, "Geronimo," then flopped onto his belly and went over.

For the first half of the hill, he looked great; going straight, keeping his knees bent and his toes up so they didn't drag, but all at once he began to swerve and I could tell right away he was overcorrecting his steering—once, twice, three times—until his feet were bouncing, kicking up puffs of snow, completely out of control. The sled took my father vaulting over the snow-hidden curb, headfirst into the trunk of a massive pin oak.

The injury didn't kill my father, although at first I thought it had when I rushed to where he lay. He was unmoving, half on, half off the sled, next to the bark-gouged oak. He somehow managed to get to his feet so that Mickey and I could each take hold of an arm to guide him back to the house. A massive purple bump jutted from his head above his right eye. When my father tried to speak his words were unintelligible. Our mother called an ambulance and my father spent almost two weeks in the hospital. X-rays showed that he'd cracked his skull, with a small sliver of bone piercing slightly into his brain. The doctors had a long talk with my mother who then came out and told Mickey and me that they'd decided not to risk operating, feeling that with time my father's brain would heal and he would return to normal. He never did, deteriorating slowly over the next six months, draining the family's finances along with my mother's usual ebullience, until one night he simply stopped breathing as the rest of us slept.

Like most ten-year-olds, I was ignorant of the fragile threads that had been holding our family together. But death's biggest irony is that it is the thing that most sharply illuminates life. I lost my innocence in earnest that cold, white February; after the ambulance came and the paramedics lifted my father's limp body onto the stretcher, and the blood-stained snow that was still beside the oak tree which Mickey and I found ourselves staring at the next day when we headed outdoors to escape the gloom which had arrived at our house.

The night our father died, my mother sat us boys down to explain how different our lives were going to be from then on. "Your father's gone, and he's not ever coming back," she said, as if we had no clue what death was. She went on about how she wasn't sure how much life insurance my father had, or how long it would last, and that she was going to have to go back to work, but that it wouldn't be easy to find a job, and that we might have to sell the house and move. The whole time she spoke, she rubbed her palms against her thighs and stared at a spot somewhere behind Mickey and me, and it dawned on me how really scared she was, for herself, and I had to fight hard not to cry.

For the first few weeks after my father's death, the three of us were like the pioneers circling our Conestogas against sudden and unforeseen Indian attacks. It was the closest I would ever feel to my mother and brother, and I have many times wished it had lasted longer. I was sad and confused by my father's death and I drew inward to find comfort in what remained of our family, understanding in some fundamental way, even at ten, that life is for the living.

Although I can never know how different things would have been without my father's absence—who knows, after all, how the world would be if Lincoln had skipped the play that evening, or Lee Harvey Oswald had been a crummy shot—many times over the years I have wondered whether Mickey and I would have made the same choices. By the end of the first month following Dad's death, Mickey had become a moody recluse, coming home from school and shutting himself in his room, often not bothering to come down to dinner. My mother fretted about him, but she was too busy trying to get our lives back on track to concern herself with a temperamental teenager. One day she told us that her sister, my Aunt Dot, had pulled some strings to get her a job in a furniture-making plant in North Carolina where Dot was an assistant manager. And when our mother announced that we'd be moving down there at the end of the school year, things only got worse with Mickey.

For my part, I was glad to be leaving Connecticut and Shaker Road and, most of all, the house in which every corner, every inch, seemed to be infected with the ghost of my father.

Early September in North Carolina, at least in High Point, was still hot and buggy, and we might just as well have been on a different planet, not just in a different state, from Connecticut. I liked it immediately. But the aspects that appealed to me most— the way complete strangers said hello in stores, the unhurried cadence of their speech, the strong sense of community— seemed to be the very things that irritated Mickey and pushed him even farther away from our family.

With the clarity of hindsight, I know the divergent paths that Mickey and I chose were simply opposite escape routes from the wretched oak on Shaker Road. I buried myself in school, becoming an A student, setting goals of achievement and potential I felt certain would have made my father proud and would honor his memory; Mickey became the troublemaker who skipped school on a regular basis and snuck booze when our mother was too busy to notice, and who was always getting detention for fighting. He and my mother would argue about his behavior and his lack of effort in school, and after a while I stopped trying to mediate these bouts and would simply wait for the door slam and soft crying that signaled a round was over.

My mother, Mickey and I stumbled along this way for several years, each hiding in our own chosen shelters of work, study or

delinquency. Then came a year of transition. It was my first
year of high school and Mickey's last. While the changes in my
brother certainly hadn't occurred overnight, the passing of time
has focused them in my mind to one event—Mickey got a
haircut. Until then, he hadn't cut his hair since we'd moved to
North Carolina. It had been the source of many disputes
between my mother and my brother, and by the time he cut it,
his hair had grown past his shoulders. But one Saturday
afternoon, Mickey walked into the kitchen where I was helping
my mother chop vegetables for dinner. The two of us turned at
the sound of the refrigerator door opening.

"We're almost out of milk," Mickey said. He closed the door
and walked out of the room.

My mother and I stared at each other, our eyes stinging from
the cut onions. I even wondered for a moment if my watery
eyes had created an optical illusion when I'd looked at my
brother. And just like that—with one simple act, one haircut—
our fractured lives showed the first real sign of healing.

What followed was, for Mickey and me at least, the longest,
dullest and most mundane period in our lives. I aced my way
through high school and went to Atlanta, to Emory University,
to study journalism. After earning my degree, I stayed in Georgia
to take a position in the metro news department of the *Macon
Telegraph*. As for Mickey, he started—and dropped out of—two
colleges before I even finished high school. He managed,
however, to pick up enough knowledge from his computer
courses to land a decent job with a budding IT firm in
Greensboro. He married a pretty, bright co-worker and they
settled into a small house that was less than ten minutes from
our mother's.

For my part, I married twice, had a daughter, and settled in
Tampa where I eventually became the Operations Director at
the *Tribune*.

My mother was in a car accident in which she smacked her
head hard against the steering wheel, but from which, unlike

my father's head trauma, she recovered completely, save for a lingering difficulty in pronouncing words beginning with "sp."

But upon reflection, I have to think this story really begins about two years ago, and started with a simple phone call from Mickey.

"Hey, Tom-Tom."

Even if I hadn't immediately recognized his deep, scratchy voice, I'd have known it was Mickey: he's the only person who calls me Tom-Tom. Once a year, he and his wife, Kelly, would come down to Florida for a long weekend and we'd all go out on a boat to fish, or head to Pelican Cove to swim in the Gulf, before spending evenings grilling steaks or shrimp and drinking beer. In between these visits we'd keep in touch by phone every couple of months.

"How are you, Mick?" I said, leaning my elbow on the kitchen table, pinching the phone against my ear, so I could sit and drink my coffee.

"Not bad. You?"

I heard a shriek from upstairs, followed by prolonged giggling. It was Sunday morning and Kylie, my nine-year-old, was having a sleepover. Her bedroom was directly above the kitchen and seven girls were running around up there, creating a low rumble in the ceiling.

"I'm good. I've got some news."

I waited.

"Kelly and I have left North Carolina and moved up north. We just bought a house."

"Up north? Where?"

"Connecticut, if you can believe that. I guess life's a big circle, right?"

I had lived nearly three-fourths of my life outside Connecticut, but even thirty years later, hearing about it made me uneasy. I sat in my kitchen in Florida, my cellphone pulled slightly away from my ear as if it would burn me, and fought the unbidden image of my father lying face down in the snow. A loud bump above me pulled me back.

"Why Connecticut?" I asked.

"Just a fluke. My boss in Greensboro was recently promoted to regional vice president at the new headquarters in Bristol. He asked me to come along to head the technical services division. It's a fantastic opportunity, with a hefty pay increase. I could hardly turn it down."

"That's great, Mickey. Congratulations."

"Thanks, but you haven't heard the weirdest part yet." Mickey paused, allowing the drama of the moment to build. I took a sip of coffee, but it hurt my stomach, so I pushed the mug across the table. "Guess what house we bought."

Of course I didn't need to ask. I sat there in the kitchen, listening half to the squeals and bangs from Kylie's room and half to Mickey's story of how, on their first house-hunting trip after accepting the job, he decided to show Kelly the town where we'd grown up, which was only fifteen minutes from Bristol. The first thing he noticed as they drove past our old house was the For Sale sign. On a whim, he dialed the number on the sign and the realtor met my brother and his wife within twenty minutes. By that evening, their offer had been accepted and the paperwork started.

"Isn't that wild?" Mickey asked.

I thought the question was rhetorical, but when Mickey didn't say anything else, I realized he wanted me to answer. "That's unexpected, all right. But what about Mom? She'll be all alone in North Carolina."

"I've talked to her about selling her house, too, and moving in with us," Mickey said. "Unless you want her to come down and live with you?"

While I had been closer to our mother when I was a teenager, Mickey, by virtue of living so close for all these years, had developed a special relationship with her. I just kept creeping south.

"No, she'd be happier with you and Kelly."

"Funny, that's what she said, too," he said.

"She did?"

Mickey laughed. "Relax, Tom-Tom, I'm only kidding. Truth is, she seems determined to stay in North Carolina as long as possible."

"Well, I can understand that."

"Yeah, me too. We'll just have to see," he said. "So, anyway, the reason I'm calling is that Kelly and I want you, Val, and Kylie to fly up for the Fourth of July weekend. I'm going to bring Mom up too."

"I don't know, Mickey, that's only three weeks away. We've talked about taking the boat down to the Keys."

"Come on, man. After all the times we drove down to visit you guys, it's payback time."

I knew he was right. And Val and I had talked only tentatively about the trip to Key West. "I'd love to, Mick, it's just that I'll have to talk it over with the girls."

"I'm not taking no for an answer. You just better start packing. Speaking of which, I gotta go *un*pack boxes. Call me next week," Mickey said, and hung up.

I sat there with the phone still at my ear, listening to the eerie silence of the broken connection, and I could feel the slight pressure in my forehead that signaled the beginning of a headache. Upstairs, the laughing and screaming intensified and, for a second, I wondered where Val was, until I remembered she was down in the basement, drying and folding bathing suits. I sat in the kitchen, my phone suspended halfway between the table and my ear for I don't know how long, but when I finally put it down and sipped my coffee it was ice cold.

I'd been thinking about the bomb my brother had just dropped on me. I knew Val would say we needed to go, that Mickey was right: we owed them a visit. And Kylie would be so excited to see her uncle, whom she adored. For someone who had never had children and always professed to never want any,

Mickey was great with kids; better, I often thought, than I was. Ever since Kylie could walk, whenever my brother saw her, he'd pretend to pull a quarter from behind her ear. Kylie would shout and jump around and act amazed, even after she learned a couple of years back that it was just a stupid old trick. The same trick, in fact, our father would play on Mickey and me on a regular basis.

Then it occurred to me how much my brother and father were alike in other ways. Physically, Mickey was the spitting image of our old man, while I took after our mother. The gravelly voice I used to think my father had acquired after years of cigarettes and booze was clearly a product of genetics, because Mickey never smoked, and drank only socially. And now, it seemed, their histories even shared real estate.

"Did somebody die?"

I hadn't heard Val come into the kitchen. "What?" I said, then stood and walked over to rinse out my coffee mug. "No, no, I just finished talking to Mickey."

"Is he okay?"

"He's fine. In fact, he called to tell me he got a nice promotion, and that he and Kelly have just bought a house." I wasn't ready to tell her which house.

"That's great news."

"Yeah. He wants us to come up for the Fourth."

"That sounds nice. It'd be good to get out of Florida for a change."

At that point, Kylie and her friends bounded into the kitchen. "Daddy, will you make French toast for us? Pleeease?"

"Of course he will," Val said, giving me a sly look. "Won't you, sweetheart?"

"I'd love to," I said.

I walked over to the refrigerator and took out the milk and eggs and placed them on the counter. Val handed me a bowl, then gave me a quick kiss on the cheek before heading out of the kitchen. I cracked half a dozen eggs into the bowl. As I poured milk on top of them, I stared at the stream. *White as Connecticut snow.* I whisked the eggs and milk with seven little girls watching and my headache worsened.

Up until two days before we were to fly to Connecticut, I was convinced that I would come up with a plausible reason why we couldn't go. Surely, I told myself, there would be some crisis at the paper requiring me to stay in Tampa, or perhaps I would get sick at the last minute and be unable to travel. To that end I even did stupid things, like stand in the shower with the water as hot as I could take it and then suddenly crank the faucet the other way until the water was ice cold, thinking the sudden chill would somehow play havoc with my immune system and thus render me susceptible to viruses. But I was cursed with good health and so found myself loading the last of the suitcases into our minivan in the gauzy predawn darkness, while Kylie fought a battle between excitement and sleepiness and Val fretted about forgetting something.

Wednesday evening we flew into Bradley International outside Hartford and Mickey and Kelly were there waiting as we deplaned. Throughout his life Mickey's demeanor had always retained vestiges of the sullen delinquent he was as a teenager, but when I saw him waving wildly to us as we walked toward the security barrier, I was struck most by how genuinely happy he looked. I don't remember ever seeing him like that. And I think what surprised me most was how good it looked on him.

"Wait'll you see the house. It looks almost exactly the same," Mickey said as we tossed the luggage into the back of his Suburban.

I wanted to tell him that, yes, I *could* wait. In fact, if we could skip the whole going-to-the-house part, it'd be just fine with me. Instead, I nodded and climbed into the front passenger seat, the girls already ensconced in the back. During the thirty-minute drive to New Britain, with the last of the day's light fading, Mickey played the role of tour guide for Val and Kylie.

He pointed out sites from our childhood that he deemed important—the road to Williston Pond, where I'd almost drowned when I was five; the park beside Dead Wood Swamp, where our family had gone for many picnics (and where, Mickey volunteered, he and Nancy Witherow shared their first-ever kiss); the entrance to the county landfill, which had had a brief moment of fame in the early '70s, when the bullet-riddled body of a Mafia informant was scooped up by a bulldozer—but I paid little attention to the places he mentioned. My mind had already driven on ahead, to Shaker Road.

"How's Mom doing?" I asked when there was a break in the travelogue. Two days earlier, Mickey had gone down to North Carolina to drive her up for the weekend.

"Same as always," Mickey said. "You know Mom; if she doesn't have something nice to say, she says it twice as loud to make sure you hear it." He looked at me and grinned, raising his eyebrows as if to say, "What're you gonna do?"

When at last Mickey turned the car onto Shaker, it was full dark and the houses lining it were only indistinct shadows, like muggers lining a dangerous alleyway. The SUV bumped into the driveway, the headlights splaying across the front of the house, and I realized Mickey was right. The house looked just as it did when I was ten. Only smaller. After a moment, the curtains in the big front window fluttered and I saw my mother squinting out, holding back the thick drapes much the way my father had done minutes before he'd insisted on borrowing my Flexible Flyer.

"Grandma!" Kylie jumped out of the Suburban and raced to the front door. The rest of us got out, and as Val and Kelly followed her up the short walk, Mickey and I went to the back to get our luggage.

I grabbed my own suitcase and Kylie's Hello Kitty backpack, then stepped back to let Mickey get the remaining two pieces. As I waited, I turned to look down Shaker Road, down the long hill toward the oak tree. I couldn't see it, but I felt its presence nonetheless. Behind me, Mickey slammed shut the car's hatch, and I jumped.

"You okay?"

"I'm fine," I said. "Let's go in so I can listen to Mom tell me that I've lost too much weight."

When we entered the house, I was instantly overwhelmed by an odd, conflicted mix of familiarness and novelty. Visually the living room in which we stood was the same as I remembered (even the somewhat eerie way Mickey and Kelly had placed their new furniture in the same pattern my parents had), yet it seemed tiny, nearly claustrophobic. I reasoned this was a common misperception of adults visiting sites of their childhood, but despite this understanding, I found myself too aware of my breathing. But something else, an odor I couldn't quite place, seemed to have lingered in the house for all these years.

"Daddy, did you hear me?" Kylie said, appearing out of nowhere and jerking my hand to get my attention.

"No, sweetie. What is it?"

"Grandma says she has a present for me." Kylie made an exaggerated expression of sadness and turned it toward my mother. "But I can't have it until after dinner."

"Oh, you'll survive, Kylie," my mother said, then looked up at me. "Don't you have a hug for your old mother, Tommy?"

I put the bags on the floor and went over to her. As I held her and kissed her cheek, I was surprised to smell the faint, oaky smell of wine on her breath. My mother almost never drank alcohol when I was a child, which, I always suspected, was to balance out my father's alcoholism so we could say that, on average, our parents were moderate drinkers. Since her car accident, however, she had developed a surprising fondness for chardonnay.

"Won't Valerie feed you?" she said as we pulled apart.

"Mom, I've gained almost ten pounds in the past year." I grabbed a hunk of my midsection for effect.

"Well, I've cooked a nice dinner, and there's plenty for everyone to have all they want."

It was then I became aware of the smell that had teased my memory when I walked into the house. Corned beef and cabbage. My father's favorite and my mother's specialty. I tilted my head and sniffed deeply.

"I should've guessed you'd cook corned beef," I said.

"She's been cooking all day," Kelly said, coming up beside me.

"Of course I have," my mother said. "I have my two boys together for the first time in a long while. That calls for a schp . . . schp . . . sssch . . ." My mother's face tightened as she concentrated on saying the word. This made her mouth tighten to a small "o" that pulsed in and out. "Ssschp-eecial meal," she managed at last. The effort left her face red and I couldn't help but think how old she looked at that moment.

"Well, Tommy," Kelly said, "while I help Mom with dinner, why don't you show Val and Kylie the house you grew up in?"

"I grew up in North Carolina," I said, too quickly. "I only lived in this house about six years. I hardly remember this place, to be honest." I glanced at Mickey, who nodded, and I knew he saw right through me.

"I'll give them a tour," Mickey announced. "Tom-Tom would leave out the good parts, anyway. Like all the places where I pinned him down and made him cry uncle."

My sister-in-law and my mother headed toward the back of the house to the kitchen, and Mickey led the rest of us upstairs to the bedrooms. I held back a moment before following, turning slowly in a circle to take in the living room one more time, alone. I had a brief sensation of being a time traveler (the heroic scientist sent back to correct a horrible wrong?), but the feeling faded quickly. I picked up my suitcase and Kylie's backpack, glanced at the big window, whose drapes blocked the darkness outside, then hurried to catch up with my family.

Thursday morning I awoke in the same bedroom I'd slept in when I was ten. Since they had no children, Mickey and Kelly had converted my old room into a home office, but it had a sleep sofa for use when the guest bedroom (Mickey's former room) was being used, like now. I shifted my back to relieve the pressure of the metal rod poking through the thin mattress, and let my eyes wander around the room. Mickey had not gotten around to hanging anything on the walls, but I readily recalled which one had my Red Sox pennants on it. In the corner to my right, next to the room's sole window, which looked out on the backyard, I had always stored my baseball bat (wooden, it being the pre-aluminum days) with my glove and cap hooked onto the end.

Next to me, Val shifted and moaned, and I knew she would be awake soon. I slid out of bed and tiptoed over Kylie, who was on the floor at the foot of the bed in a sleeping bag. On the way downstairs I could smell coffee brewing and hear someone moving about. When I shuffled into the kitchen, my mother was organizing everything she'd need to make breakfast. She didn't hear me at first and I stood quietly, watching her for several moments. At sixty-eight, and despite the injury, she still looked vigorous. And even though her hair was now silver and short instead of brown and long, looking from behind, seeing her standing in this kitchen about to cook breakfast, I again had that eerie feeling of distant familiarity.

"Expecting to feed an army?" I asked, walking over and kissing her cheek. Beside the stovetop were two cartons of a dozen eggs each, and the largest package of bacon I'd ever seen.

"It's been a long time since I had my whole family together, Mr. Smart-Mouth, so don't go poking fun. You know I always liked to cook breakfast for you boys. So just get yourself some coffee and sit down and let me sp-sp-spoi-oi . . . spoil you like when you were young, Thomas."

As I always had, I obeyed my mother. I poured some coffee and sat at the kitchen table. I was filled with the memory of when I was in high school, when Mom and I were the close ones, and Mickey was the outsider. My mother slit the bacon wrapper and separated some strips, which she laid into a skillet.

Almost immediately I could smell the comforting smell of the meat and hear the sizzle as she scooted the strips into a line. I heard the muffled sound of a toilet flushing upstairs.

"Can I ask you something, Mom?" I asked, knowing our time alone was about up.

"Why do you think Mickey bought this house?"

My mother didn't turn and look at me, but I noticed the arm that had been moving the bacon around stopped moving for a moment.

"I guess it reminds him of happy childhood memories," she said. "Keep in mind, Tommy, that he lived here three years longer than you did."

"I know, but . . ."

My mother turned and looked directly at me. I knew then that coming here, to this house, had been as difficult for her as it was for me, and what I felt at that moment wasn't sadness but relief.

"Mickey has always been able to look at the big picture," she said, turning back to the stove and her cooking. "I'm old, but I'm not stupid, Tommy. I know how hard it is for you to be here. But don't forget how difficult it was for your brother right after your father's accident. It took him a good while to work through it, but eventually he did. And in my own way, I have, too. Ever since we left Connecticut all those years ago, you have been running farther and farther away from it, from this place."

I started to take a sip of coffee but put the cup down. "It was so . . . avoidable. That's what haunts me, Mom. I knew he was too old—"

"You mean too *drunk*," she said, looking over her shoulder at me.

"Maybe both. I just shouldn't have let him do it."

"Let who do what?" Val asked, walking into the room.

I rarely mentioned my father around my wife, especially about the circumstances of his death, and I was trying to think of how to answer when my mother spoke.

"Oh, your silly husband is saying he should have paid for airplane tickets so I could fly up here instead of letting Mickey drive all the way down to get me. Now, how do you like your eggs, Valerie dear?"

I listened as my wife and my mother chattered about cooking and Kylie and shopping and probably a dozen other things I didn't hear. All I kept thinking about was what she had said to me, about running away.

During breakfast, Mickey mentioned that his firm paid for membership at a small country club in nearby Farmington, and that he'd arranged a 10:30 tee time for us. Before that, however, he had to run over to his office in Bristol to clear some things from his desk before the long weekend. He invited me to tag along, but I declined. Kelly was going to take Val, Kylie and my mother into New York for a day of shopping and sightseeing. So, unexpectedly, a few minutes after nine o'clock, I found myself alone in the house.

Whenever I'm visiting other cities, I like to check out the local paper, the competition if you will. So I sat in the living room, scanning the *Hartford Courant*—not so much to read the news, but to compare the layout and organization of the paper to that of my own. The house faced east, so the early morning sun poured through the picture window, reflecting off the pages, nearly blinding me. I walked over to close the drapes. When I grabbed the curtain, a car drove by, drawing my attention to the street. Then it hit me that I was standing in the same spot, looking out at the same road, as my father had mere moments before he'd come out to demand a turn on my sled. I turned my head to the right, to gaze down the hill of Shaker Road. And, of course, it was still there.

The oak of my childhood had, over the years, achieved redwood status in my aging memory. But now it seemed, I noted sadly from my vantage point at the window, rather small as trees go. A pathetic tree, even. I started to wonder if I was mistaking this fairly meager trunk for the same one that had put an abrupt end to my father's sledding adventure, altering our lives forever.

When I let go of the curtains my hand was slick with sweat, which I wiped on my shorts. I opened the front door and stepped outside. The early morning air was already hot, presaging a stifling day. But standing on the small porch, my mind easily conjured up a vision of a snow-blanketed town, our walkway dotted by Mickey's and my boot prints. I cut across the postage-stamp lawn and down the sidewalk, my pace slowing as I got nearer to the oak tree. When I reached it, my hands were again moist with sweat, but this time I saw no point in wiping them off.

I don't know how long I stood in that spot, staring at that tree, but I do remember eventually moving around so that I was in the street, facing the tree from the direction that the sled carrying my father had chosen. And what struck me in that moment was not what I was seeing—a common tree that had altered my life forever—but what I did not see. I studied the oak high and low for some scar, some nick, that served as a permanent reminder of my foolish choice to hand the sled's towrope to my father. But the tree's rough, cracked bark was unblemished in any way that would show the world the result of its unforgiving hardness.

I somehow managed to start walking away, but heard a loud crunch under my sandal. At my feet were dozens of acorns, two of which had been crushed by my shoe. I picked up an intact one and rolled it around on my palm. *Mighty oaks from little acorns grow.* I shook my head at the old axiom, then walked back to the house, absently pocketing the acorn as I opened the door.

All that day, I found myself thinking about the oak tree on Shaker Road. I couldn't concentrate on my golf game, finishing eighteen strokes behind Mickey. After lunch I tried to nap, but only tossed and turned on the living room sofa. In the evening, as Mickey and I grilled burgers and hotdogs for dinner, I struggled to pay attention as Kylie told me about her exciting ferry ride to visit the Statue of Liberty, and all the huge department stores she had seen.

"You're awfully quiet, Tommy," my mother said, walking up with a small plate of sliced cheese.

"He's just not used to all this leisure time," Mickey said. "You know what a workaholic he is." He took the cheese from her and began laying the slices on top of the burgers.

"You just need to clear your mind, relax, and have a good time," my mother said. "That stupid old newspaper ran just fine before you were there, and it'll run long after you're gone." She reached over and squeezed my arm. "Life goes on with or without us, dear. We need to just enjoy the time we have and stop worrying about things we can't change."

I started to say that she sounded like my father giving one of his frequent spur-of-the-moment sermons, but nodded instead.

"By the way," my mother said, "Kylie wanted me to ask you if she could light some of her sp . . . schpaa . . . sp-sp-sparklers tonight when it gets dark. I assured her that you would say yes." She smiled, and I couldn't help reciprocating.

"In that case, I think it would be fine," I said.

"Good. Then it's settled."

"Who's hungry?" Mickey said, hoisting a platter of steaming cheeseburgers.

We all sat around the patio, talking about the simple things that families talk about when they get together, avoiding the big things we probably should talk about, and I ate very little.

Shortly before midnight, everyone else in the house was asleep. I shifted and rolled around but couldn't get comfortable on the sofa bed. While my thoughts would always circle back to the oak tree outside just down the road, my mind chased a phantom that had crept in sometime after I had come inside from confronting the tree that morning.

Unable to sleep, I slipped out of bed and headed downstairs. I went into the kitchen and walked over to the door that led to the basement. There was no chance, I knew, of finding what I was looking for, but I flicked on the light and went down.

In all the intervening years, and intervening owners, no one had seen fit to finish the basement. It was, I realized, too small to use for anything but storage. The two dim light bulbs created pockets of shadow in each corner of the damp cellar. I walked around the basement like a visitor to a museum, looking for anything that could be deemed interesting. In the far corner, Mickey and Kelly had stacked several boxes marked Winter Clothing. I checked behind them, but what I was looking for was not there. I looked in each corner, behind the water heater and furnace, but found nothing. I'd known all along that I would not find the Flexible Flyers, but knew, too, that I had to be certain. I started up the stairs, feeling a strange mixture of relief and disappointment, when my eyes caught a glimpse of something wooden through the open spaces between the steps. I had not looked under the stairs. Goosebumps rose on my arms as I went back downstairs. Surely, I told myself, our sleds could not have stayed hidden under the basement stairs for all these years. But I had to see for myself.

Of course the sleds were not there. Through the stairs I had spotted the wooden handles of old tools. And while I registered the variety of them—sledgehammer, hoe, shovel—I could not take my eyes off the nearest one, a large ax. I took the ax, much heavier than I expected, and carried it upstairs and out the front door.

I went into the street and down the hill to the oak tree, hopping a couple times as I stepped on acorns with my bare feet. The air was still warm even in the middle of the night, but cool in comparison to the sweltering heat of the day and that coolness made me think of winter and snow. When I reached the oak tree, I never paused, never hesitated; simply lifted the ax and swung it as hard as I could. After the first few strokes, small chips of wood from the trunk were flying around me. The jagged wedge I created grew like a slow grin, mocking me, so I swung faster and faster. The earthy scent of fresh-cut wood filled my head. Then I heard a distant shrill of a siren, and beneath it a low voice; a voice that sounded just like my father's but was my own, shouting, screaming unintelligible words.

I don't know how long Mickey, Kelly, Val and my mother stood on the dark sidewalk with a small gathering of curious neighbors , watching me flail at the tree, begging me to put the ax down. I finally felt a heavy ache in my shoulders and stopped to rest. Mickey rushed over and pulled the tool from my hands. I made a half-hearted effort to get it back, but I knew I was done. I looked at the trunk of the oak tree and saw the jagged gash I had made. It was far from enough to topple or kill the tree, but I felt satisfaction that it would at least now bear the scar it should have borne for thirty years.

My mother and Val, both crying, guided me back toward the house. A police car pulled up, lights flashing, and when my wife and mother led me into the house, Mickey was still pointing to the tree, explaining to the officer what had happened.

I wish that I could tell you that my rampage on Shaker Road was the catharsis I needed to put my father's death, and my guilt associated with it, finally to rest. But all it showed me was that exorcising my demons was not going to be as simple as cutting down an old oak tree in suburban Connecticut. We ended our visit early and flew back to Tampa the following day. When I unpacked my luggage, sorting my clean clothes from my used ones, I discovered the acorn I'd put in the pocket of my shorts. For several weeks it sat, untouched, on my dresser. Then one Saturday, while Val and Kylie were out of the house, I buried it in the sandy dirt of our backyard. I harbor no illusions it will grow in Florida, but at least it's out of sight.

Next month, Val, Kylie and I are moving yet again, this time down to Miami, where I've accepted a job at the *Herald*, even though it involves a pay cut. I am running out of land, so I hope that this time I can outrun my father's phantom who, I have come to learn, is no one's but my own. I'm not so naïve that I believe I will. But I do take comfort in knowing that, as winter fast approaches, here there will be no snow.

Getting the Message

After she has left her apartment to go to The Flaming Wok to pick up their carryout, he ambles into the kitchen for a beer. As he looks about the room, it dawns on him that it is the first time he's been alone in her place. In the past three months, since he has been coming there, he has become comfortable, but their time has been spent mostly in the bedroom.

She is a doctor, a surgeon, and her kitchen reflects an orderly precision he assumes she brings to her work. The stainless steel pots and pans that hang in a row, in descending order of size, gleam under bright fluorescents. When he opens the refrigerator, there's a puff of cool, citrus-scented air across his face and arms, and he notes that the refrigerator's contents—jars of relish and mayonnaise and olives, storage containers with carefully saved leftovers, a carton of 2% milk—appear thoughtfully arranged for easy retrieval. Four bottles of Corona are lined up like soldiers along the top shelf. He grabs the second one from the left, and the gap it leaves seems glaring.

Her phone rings, startling him, and he closes the refrigerator. He wonders if she is calling him with some question about his order—was it steamed rice or fried?—so he walks back into the living room toward the phone. Just as it rings for the third time, he reaches for it, but stops. No, he thinks. She would call his cell phone. He listens as the fourth ring is cut off by the answering machine.

The greeting is short, to the point, and is, he realizes again, so like her. At its conclusion, a female voice, made slightly tinny the way all voices are changed by these machines, begins to leave a message. In a trick of the mind, he conjures an imagined face for the voice (not too young, dark hair cut short, wide intelligent eyes) as he stands listening while it is recorded. The unopened beer bottle sweats onto his hand.

"Hey, sorry I missed your call. I've been thinking about what you said and, as much as I hate to agree, you're right that this is only headed for trouble. When any married man, even one who's separated, tells you that you need to be patient so he can resolve things, then he's in no hurry to get a divorce. I'm sorry, sweetie, but you two do need to have the talk. Anyway, call me when you get in. Bye."

The final word hangs in the air and lodges in his head, which begins to feel heavy. He had thought it odd that she wanted to get together tonight, on such short notice, but assumed, in his arrogance, that she missed him as much as he did her. He thinks about the weekend just past. They had driven out of the city, to a secluded spot by the river he knew well, and there they had a picnic, lying in the dappled sunlight beneath a tall oak, embracing until they rolled off the blanket onto the cool grass, where they undressed each other and wrestled and laughed with a soft breeze blowing off the water, chilling their sweat-slicked skin. Afterward, they pulled on their clothes and he kissed her. The bliss he felt was enormous, seeming to fill every cell of his body. He'd whispered to her: "This is what I've been searching for."

After several minutes, he goes again to the kitchen, where he replaces the beer in its place in line. When he walks back into the living room, he stares down at the blinking light on the answering machine, and he is filled with an emptiness that is surprising in its heft, like a lead ball in his gut.

He hears her fighting the key into the door lock. He imagines her in the hallway, balancing cartons of hot and sour soup and jumbo shrimp as she fiddles with it. He will go and help her with her burden, even though he has lost his appetite, but before he goes to her, he reaches down to press the button that erases the message.

WHO'S THE VICTIM HERE?

When I was very young, I collided with things so frequently—tripping over furniture, running into trees while playing outside, banging into door jambs instead of navigating around them—that it became obvious to my mother that I had a vision problem. The day before my fifth birthday, she took me to the doctor, who diagnosed me with what he called a "lazy eye," and told my mother that it could be corrected with surgery, followed by a few months in which I'd have to wear a patch over my good eye, the right one, to strengthen the weak muscles of my left while they healed. One of my most vivid childhood memories is of my parents arguing about my operation.

"That's too much money," my father had yelled when my mother told him how much the surgery cost.

We lived in a tiny house with thin walls, and I lay in my bedroom listening to them argue in the living room downstairs.

"We're talking about his eyesight, for God's sake," my mother shouted back.

"You said the other eye is normal, right? Lots of people can't see out of *either* eye. He should count his blessings."

I can't remember how long they fought, just that it ended, as it did so often, with my mother, in tears, running upstairs and locking herself in the bathroom. In the end, I had the operation, but hated wearing the sticky, rough patch over my good eye because I couldn't watch TV, so whenever my mother wasn't around I'd peel it up so I could see. Forty years later, I can barely see out of my left eye.

As I grew older, I adapted to the slight loss of depth perception my condition caused, although there were certain things that I would never be very good at, like catching a ball. My father, who'd lettered in baseball and football in high school, lost an opportunity to go to college on a baseball scholarship because his grades were so poor. He was not a tall man, but was broad and muscular with dramatic facial features—bright blue eyes set deep under a prominent ridge of forehead, a large, bulbous nose, thick black hair. In his fantasy, I had inherited his innate skill and would someday fulfill his lost potential. But by the time I reached middle school, I had grown into a tall, gangly teenager and it was apparent to both of us that I would never succeed in sports, something he blamed on a lack of effort, not my lack of visual acuity. I was, it seems, a disappointment years in the making.

In hindsight, an uneasy peace existed in our house most of the time, punctuated by occasional skirmishes between my mother and father. For my part, I laid low, hiding in my room after school. In my solitude, I found other role models to spend my time with, and from whom I could learn about life. While my father could unhesitatingly quote statistics about Mantle or Killebrew or Yastrzemski, I could as eloquently quote Salinger or London or Steinbeck.

After my parents' divorce, my father rented a one-bedroom apartment in the northeastern corner of our hometown of Eden, North Carolina. His apartment was in the Beerville section, so-called because the small cluster of frame houses and garden apartments abutted the property of the Miller Brewing Plant, which was separated only by a single row of tall, scraggly pine trees. As part of the divorce settlement, I spent one weekend a month with my father. Every time I visited his "bachelor pad," the aroma of hops was so overwhelming I swore I could taste it on my tongue.

Our weekends together were awkward for both of us. Friday evenings, I climbed into his 1971 mustard-colored Gremlin (taking care not to bunch up whatever towel he'd placed on the passenger seat to cover the long rip in the stained fabric) and, invariably, the first thing he'd do is ask me about girls.

"Dating any cute cheerleaders?" This was one of his favorite opening lines.

"No, but this week I was elected vice president of the Literature Club. It's the first time a freshman's held the position."

My father's head swiveled back and forth, looking from me to the road to me again, perhaps trying to determine if I was kidding.

"*Literature?*" he said. "As in book-reading literature?"

"Yeah, Dad. We select a classic novel, and then after everyone's read it, we discuss it."

"No offense, son, but it sounds like a club for girls. Or faggots."

"Well, why on earth would I take offense at *that?*" I said, and then turned to look out my window, wishing like hell it was already Sunday.

When we got to his place, my father would boil us some hot dogs and tear open a bag of potato chips and we'd sit in front of the TV watching *Miami Vice*, washing our dinner down with Cheerwine or Mountain Dew. More often than not, my father fell asleep before the show ended. Whenever he did, I was relieved that we were spared the angst of trying to hold a conversation.

Saturdays were the toughest. Some weekends, my father, who was a security guard for a large textile plant, had to work the morning shift, from six to noon. While he was gone, I did my homework or read, trying to tune out the near-constant rumble and rattle of beer trucks pulling in and out of the brewery next door. If my father wasn't working, or after he got home from work, he'd try to find some activity to entertain me. Often, he'd suggest things like miniature golf or bowling or the movies, and it always made me feel like I was ten years old again. But I never said anything. I went along with whatever activity he picked, knowing in my heart that it was just a way to kill time for both of us.

In the spring, if the weather was warm, my father and I drove down to Greensboro on Saturday afternoon to watch a baseball game. I've never been a sports fan and I found baseball particularly boring, but the worst part was the forty-five minutes trapped in the car on the drive to and from the stadium. I'd learned as a young boy not to argue with my father, no matter how wrong I knew him to be. His temper lay beneath the surface of his personality like a lion hiding in the grass, waiting to pounce on small or weak prey that happened to cross its path. As we drove toward the ball field, he'd scream at other drivers he deemed incompetent, particularly if they had the gall to pass us. "Numb nut" was his favorite epithet for these drivers, and was, to my mind, his highway mantra. Unless, of course, the driver happened to be black, then he or she was a "numb-nut nigger."

During my sophomore year, I turned sixteen and obtained my driver's license. On those weekends that I had to spend with my father, my mother loaned me her car so that I could drive myself to Beerville. Ostensibly, this was a reward for getting good grades, but I suspected it was more for me to have freedom to come and go as I wanted. Even though I knew it meant my mother would have to ride the bus on her errands, I didn't put up a fight. I was glad, and more than a little grateful.

As that summer approached, there was a rash of burglaries in my father's part of town. Houses and apartments were broken into, sometimes during the day, sometimes at night, and the thief or thieves typically stole cash or televisions or small appliances. After two weeks, the police had stepped up patrols in the area, but the crimes continued unabated. I read the brief stories about the break-ins in the local paper, but I didn't give them any more thought than I did the notices of swap meets or bake sales.

I drove to my father's apartment one unseasonably hot Friday in May, anticipating another boring evening of TV and hot dogs. My father had given me a key to his apartment for those days when he'd have to work. I never used it. The apartment was on the second floor of a four-apartment building. As I climbed the stairs, I heard the sound of a television being played extremely loud. I knew the tenant in the apartment across from my father was a long-distance truck driver who was almost never there, and as I reached the top step, I confirmed the noise was coming from my father's apartment. When I knocked, there was no response. I placed the backpack that contained my clothes and schoolbooks on the hall floor and dug into the pocket of my jeans for the key. When I unlocked the door and tried to push it open, it was stopped abruptly by the chain on the other side. My father's face appeared suddenly in the gap, startling me.

"Oh, shit. In all the excitement, I forgot you were coming," he said. "Hang on a second." He closed the door, and I could just make out his voice amid the din of the TV. After a minute, the chain rattled and the door opened halfway. "Come in, quick," my father said.

In the middle of the living room, a young black kid was sitting in one of my father's armless dinette chairs. His hands were bound behind the chair with an electrical extension cord, and his ankles were lashed to the front legs of the chair with white tube socks. The left side of the kid's face was bruised and a trickle of blood ran from his ear. His left eye was swollen shut. When I turned back toward my father, he was relocking the door. I noticed the television on the floor right next to the door, the cord stretched tight along the wall to the nearest socket. Lying next to the set was my father's radio, VCR (which hadn't worked in nearly a year), and the three folders that contained my father's prized coin collection.

"What's going on?" I asked, shouting to be heard over the noise from the TV.

My father slipped the chain lock back in place. "I came home from work and found this nigger trying to steal my stuff."

He pointed to the stash next to the door, and I put it all together. I looked at the kid and saw the terror in his one open eye, which was red from crying. A washcloth bulged from his mouth.

"Jesus Christ. What have you done?"

"Just relax, son," my father said. "I'm just teaching this little punk a lesson about stealing. That's all."

"Have you called the police?" I asked. I felt lightheaded, and for a moment I really thought I was going to faint.

The kid in the chair tried to say something, but all that came out was a high-pitched moan. My father walked over and slapped him.

"I told you not to try to talk!" my father said.

"I'm calling the cops," I said, and walked toward the phone.

"Please don't do that, son."

"Why not?"

"I'm not done teaching him right from wrong, that's why. No one steals from me and gets away with it."

"Look at his face," I shouted. "Don't you think he's learned it by now?"

The kid began nodding furiously. My father lifted his arm to strike him, but I dropped my backpack and raced over and grabbed his wrist. My father shoved me away, and I fell onto my ass.

"Damn it. Why'd you do that?" my father asked. He came over and extended his hand to help me up, but I scooted backward and stood on my own.

"Leave me alone," I said. My face felt hot.

"I'm sorry. I didn't mean to hurt you."

Across the room, through the window, I saw the lights along the roof of the Miller plant come on.

"Untie him and call the police, or I will," I said.

My father looked at the terrified burglar, and for a moment, I thought he was going to do it.

"What's wrong with you, son? You act like I'm the bad guy." He held his arms up, like I was pointing a gun at him. "Who's the victim here?"

He pointed once again to the meager pile of possessions by the door, the essence of my father's wealth, and I realized for the first time in my life that not only had my father fallen far short of any expectations he might have had in life, but that he knew it.

"I'm calling the police now," I said. "You'll already have a hard time explaining what happened to him. Don't make it worse."

"What do you mean?" my father said. "It was self-defense."

I looked at the skinny kid and then at my father who, although he'd softened with age, still looked like a retired boxer.

"Tell it to the cops."

This time my father didn't try to stop me as I walked to the phone. After making the call, I untied the kid, and my father held him by the arms until the police arrived less than five minutes later. The kid didn't try to struggle.

As soon as I gave my report to the officer and they took the kid away, I picked up my backpack and left the apartment without saying anything to my father. I drove home and told my mother that Dad's job schedule had changed permanently and that I wouldn't be going back to spend any weekends with him. I knew she was suspicious, but she never said anything.

Over the years, I'd hear from my mother whenever my father changed jobs or moved, but I had my own life to worry about— college, graduate school, a wife, a baby boy. I saw my father only once more.

A month before he died of pancreatic cancer, my father came to see me at one of my book signings in Charlotte, where I now live. The disease had taken its toll on his body. He was gaunt and walked like each step was painful. The skin of his face hung like a shirt two sizes too big. His eyes, which once had seemed intense, looked sepulchral. He tried to praise my book, which I knew he'd never read, but his words were awkward and clumsy, very much like my attempts to catch a baseball. I thanked him and shook his hand, but we didn't hug. He said he couldn't stay. I thanked him again for coming, and for one brief moment I felt uncertain and disappointed, but in whom I wasn't sure.

When my father died, my mother called to tell me that he had left me his coin collection. Had I been younger, I might have told her to just throw it away, but instead I told her I'd get it the next time I visited. My father was buried at Ridge View Cemetery in Eden, five minutes from Beerville. I didn't go up for the burial. My mother and a few people from where he worked were the only ones who showed up.

My son knows nothing of his paternal grandfather, and I know soon he'll ask about him. It's difficult to know what I'll tell him when he does, but most likely I'll say his grandfather was a pretty good athlete who could have, had he gotten a break, been a pro. And, I'll tell him, his granddad could boil a pretty mean hot dog.

June Bug

I t's the smell you remember most—soft and faint, yet powerful enough it lingers in the nose for all these years. A flower scent, but with a sharp undercurrent, cinnamon perhaps, that makes you, you this little girl, nine or ten years old, want to lean into it to pull it deep into your nostrils in order to learn it, memorize it. And lean you do, feeling the woman's arm around your shoulder to tuck you in close as she bends down to teach you about the large bug with shimmering green-blue wings inching along the railing of her front porch. Miss Crenshaw's odd, deep voice whispers close to your ear and you feel the tickle of short puffs of her breath as she tells you it's a June bug, saying it's rare to see one alone in the daylight.

This recollection is pleasant, yet never welcome. You sense the feeling that is coming, the ice ball in your core, whenever you recall the scent of Miss Crenshaw's soap and the unbidden series of images welded to it. Sweet Miss Crenshaw, who had no children of her own, but was always happy to see you playing across the street in your own front yard, telling you to ask your mother if you can come over and have a popsicle. Your disappointment when your mother says no, it'll spoil your dinner—even though you'd only just eaten lunch—but maybe next time, and to please not bother Miss Crenshaw.

But you drift across to her yard anyway when your mother is glued to the television watching her soaps, or on the back patio with her friends drinking sweaty glasses of iced tea and complaining about how their husbands don't appreciate all they do for them. Miss Crenshaw waves you over to help her repair the loose board on the porch steps, even letting you try to hammer a nail, laughing when you mess up and bend it, not getting mad at all. Patiently showing you how to use the claw to yank out your failure and then holding your hand to guide your swing straight the next time. She stands up and wipes grime off her hands onto the legs of her bell-bottom jeans, folds her arms across her white-ribbed tank top as she assesses your work. You want to imitate the action, but know your mother would have a fit if you intentionally got dirt on your dress. Miss Crenshaw asks you to jump on the step to test it. You leap up and off, up and off, up and off until you both are laughing. The board is tight. She shakes your hand and says job well done. You skip back across the street to your house. Inside, your mother is still watching TV. You start to tell her what you did but she shushes you, so you keep it to yourself.

And that summer your mother kicks you out of the house so she can clean, or so you can stay out of the way when the other women come over, and your father is gone from early morning until late (sometimes even well after supper) at his job where you don't really know what he does, so you find yourself sliding into a routine of wandering over to Miss Crenshaw's. One day she lets you help in her garden, teaching you the names of the flowers and plants and insects as you kneel beside her. Or another time she is sitting on her porch with an enormous atlas spread open on her lap, using a felt-tip marker to draw lines from the center of North Carolina to the dozen dots she's made all over Europe and Asia and South America, to the places she's been and the places she plans to visit. You listen, learning about children in Mexico who run around the city streets barefoot, begging from tourists because their parents have no money, or about the fierce wind at the top of the Eiffel Tower that blows her hat into the asparagus-colored water of the Seine, and listen in amazement at the tale of tenacious snow that lingers at the top of Mount Rainier even in mid-July.

You ask things, many things. How is it that the snow doesn't melt? The top is closer to the sun and it is the hottest month of the year. Miss Crenshaw laughs, but it is not mean, and she strokes your hair (which is as light and long as hers is dark and short), and she explains about the atmosphere and how the air is thinner and colder at the higher altitude of the mountaintop. And so you go through most of the summer this way, learning and asking and listening. It is the best summer yet.

At your age, you do not yet know about life's sometimes heartless vagaries, but discover its capricious nature that very summer while holding your mother's hand as you walk one afternoon along the row of stores at the shopping center. In a quiet moment, when your mother is staring absently at shoes through a smudged glass window, you hope to impress her with all you have learned those past weeks. And, at first, she *is* impressed. But the pride you feel is short-lived. Where did you learn all this, she asks. You tell her and soon you are back home, sitting at the top of the stairs, listening to your mother make calls to her friends, one after another. You can't hear it all, but there are things said—strange and angry words—that you don't understand.

And then you sneak downstairs to peek out from the side of the front window curtain even though your mother said to stay in your room. You watch your mother across the street talking to Miss Crenshaw on her porch. Your mother is gesturing wildly, pointing back over to your house and you wish you could see Miss Crenshaw's face, but it is blocked by your mother's body. Only when your mother is heading back, crossing the road, can you see Miss Crenshaw standing at her door, her hands on her hips, and she is looking, it seems, right at you. You hurry back to your room before the front door slams shut.

Your father comes to you later that night to tell you that you must not visit Miss Crenshaw again, but when you ask why he only says it is for your own good. Trust me and your mother to know what is best, he says. So you obey and soon school starts and one weekend a large truck is parked in front of Miss Crenshaw's house and then she is gone.

You struggle to identify what it is that happened that lazy, humid summer day, and cannot. Only that you know you had somehow started events into motion that you would take back if you could. And it bothers you enough to never leave you, even when you become old enough to understand, if not comprehend. A dreadful day which had started out so great— sipping lemonade in the shade of Miss Crenshaw's porch, humming softly as you trace circles in a thin layer of pollen dust that has settled on the green painted boards, until you notice the big bug that alights on the porch railing. You stand and approach cautiously, so as not to frighten the insect and because you are, well, a little scared yourself. What kind is it? The woman comes next to you and pulls you close to her. You get lost for a moment in the redolence of her delicate scent as she leans down and says it is a lone June bug, not common in daytime. Then she kisses the top of your head softly and tells you don't worry, it won't hurt you.

RAY MORRISON spent most of his childhood in Brooklyn, New York, and Washington, D.C., but headed south after college to earn his degree in veterinary medicine and he hasn't looked north since. He has happily settled in Winston-Salem, North Carolina, with his wife and three children where, when he is not writing short stories, he ministers to the needs of dogs, cats and rodents. His fiction has appeared in *Ecotone*, *Fiction Southeast*, *Aethlon*, *Carve Magazine*, *Word Riot*, *Night Train*, and others. His stories also appear in a number of anthologies, including *What Doesn't Kill You...*, *Press 53 Spotlight*, and *The Mix Tape: A Flash Fiction Anthology* (Fast Forward Press). He won First Prize in the Short Story category of the 2011 Press 53 Open Awards and he has twice won Honorable Mention in the Lorian Hemingway Short Story Competition.

Cover artist **JEREMY MINIARD** has his roots firmly planted in the rich soils of the rural south. Raised in the small central Alabama town of Pell City, and spending the hot dusty summers of his childhood even deeper in the ravel of the 'Bama back roads of Conecuh County, his work reflects the charm and mystery he found in his surroundings there. A building contractor by trade, he moonlights as a landscape and sports photographer. He married his former high school and college sweetheart—he a saxophonist, she a trombonist—in 2000. They now have two children who are ever his motivation. First and foremost, Jeremy enjoys spending time with his wife and children, but he also enjoys hiking, fishing, and searching for those yet unphotographed, rusty, kudzoo-covered treasures of a bygone era. He has always had a fascination with the ability a photograph has to capture a moment in time and make it last forever. See more of Jeremy's photography at www.flickr.com/photos/jwminiard/, and look for Remy Photography on Facebook.

A Note from the Author

Many people are responsible for bringing these stories life outside the confines of my imagination.

I must start by thanking Kevin Watson, my editor/publisher, for his unwavering belief in my writing and for making this book possible.

A big thank you to the members of my monthly writers' group—Bob Shar, Steve Lindahl, and Joni Bartenfield Carter—for the innumerable suggestions, corrections, and tips that shaped the sometimes ugly early drafts of many of these stories into readable fiction.

Many thanks to the editors of the literary journals who saw value in my work and published them.

The support and encouragement of my wife, Jeni Geisler, and my children, Katie, Margaret, and Yuri, cannot be overstated. They pushed me on when I wanted to give up and never doubted when I frequently did. I am a writer today because of them and, even as a writer, cannot find words to tell them how much I love and appreciate them.

CPSIA information can be obtained at www.ICGtesting.com
Printed in the USA
BVOW010223061212

307343BV00006B/1570/P